LAST OF THE SAN PATRÍCIOS

Frontispiece

LAST OF THE SAN PATRÍCIOS

a novel by

Terry Hagerty

Otherworld Cottage Industries
Los Angeles

First Printing, April 2020

Hagerty, Terry
Last of the San Patricios

    1. Historical Novel. 2. San Patricios Battalion. 3.
    I. Terry Hagerty. II. Title.

813.54

ISBN-13   978-1-892900-08-1
ISBN-10: 1892900084

Printed in the United States of America
Cover Design and Illustrations by Linda Snyder

Otherworld Cottage Industries
1746 South Kingsley Drive, Los Angeles, CA 90006

Special Thanks to:

Travis Edward Pike, my editor and publisher, for his encouragement, his patience, his insight, and his many other considerable talents.

Linda Snyder, for her brilliant cover and illustrations.

Members of the New Playwrights Foundation, for reading an early draft and giving me a great many suggestions that improved the story.

My Irish ancestors, who inspired me to delve into Gaelic culture, history, and the Irish diaspora.

CONTENTS

GLORIOSVS oriundas fuit: lt ex parenab. secundum soculi dignitace. venerandos ec religione xp̄i

Chapter One

October 28, 1879 -- California

The sight of two Franciscan friars riding into the remote California mining camp of shacks, tents, and perpetual mud puddles created more than a little curiosity and even some annoyance. After all, the intrusion of religion conflicted with the miners' usual recreational activities of liquor, gambling, and prostitutes. But for many of the Catholic miners, the chance to attend Mass and give confession after many months of religious neglect was most welcome -- even on a Tuesday.

While Father Seamus rang his copper handbell, Father Michael set up a temporary altar outside on a borrowed table, with a couple of brass candlesticks from his saddlebags and a beautiful wooden crucifix, hand-carved by a Mexican craftsman they had met several years ago in Santa Fe.

Father Seamus was a natural orator, mixing Catholic liturgy and common-sense morality, with just enough Latin

thrown in to leave the crowd feeling spiritually inspired --
inspired enough to contribute liberally to the two donation
trays Father Michael passed around (that doubled as their
supper plates).

After Mass, the two friars borrowed a small tent and
tossed a blanket over a rope tied to the tent poles at either end,
turning it into a highly serviceable confessional.

Confessions went quickly enough, with the usual list of
swearing, gambling, fighting, whoring, and drinking, though
not necessarily in that order. Numerous Hail Marys and Our
Fathers were handed out by Father Michael, while Father
Seamus stood outside and encouraged wayward Catholics to
go in and unburden their souls -- then possibly contribute a
little extra to the makeshift poor box setup outside the tent for
the particularly guilt-ridden.

The two Irishmen did quite well from this deception.
The fact that neither Sean Mulcahy nor Michael Lonergan had
ever actually been tonsured, let alone studied for the church,
didn't mean Sean didn't deliver a perfectly good Mass. His
Latin may have been thin, and probably incorrect, but the
crowds always seemed to enjoy hearing Father Seamus's
approximation of the liturgy.

And Sean looked the part. With his piecing blue eyes
and scruffy blonde beard, which did a poor job of masking the
scar on his right cheek, he looked like a man who had seen a
good deal of the world and had confronted sin on more than
one occasion. And he wore the dark brown Franciscan habit
and cowl like he was born to it.

Michael had attempted conducting Mass, but he didn't
possess Sean's theatrical inclination. He was more the quiet,
inquisitive type, with his thinning gray hair and gray beard,
that still showed traces of the dark brown of his youth, and

dark brown eyes, behind his wire-rimmed spectacles, that took in much more than one might suppose, a personality more suited to hearing confessions and granting absolutions.

They had tried their hands at a variety of other jobs through the years, most of them back-breaking and for little pay. As they grew older, they sought out less physical and, hopefully, more lucrative ways to make money. The Franciscan friar scheme seemed made to order for them. Sean could even justify it by reminding Michael how much comfort and contentment they brought to wayward Catholics in those out of the way places. Then again, Sean could talk himself into pretty much anything, and Michael usually went along -- eventually.

The pair only donned their habits and cowls just before entering a mining camp and removed them not long after they left. It wasn't appropriate apparel, if they wanted to spend their blasphemous, ill-gotten gains on a whiskey or a woman of easy virtue in another town.

Sean loved a good game of poker. He enjoyed the camaraderie and competition that came with each deal of the cards. Most of all, he enjoyed the conversation. He loved to tell a story between hands about some of the fascinating places and people he and Michael had come across in their wanderlust wanderings. Even if most of his stories were complete fabrications, they were always told with great style.

Michael enjoyed playing poker as well, but, like most things in life, he took the game a little more seriously than Sean. He didn't enter into the table conversation, concentrating on his cards and searching for any 'tells' the other players might have, which might reveal what cards they were holding.

In one particular town on the western edge of the Sierra Nevada mountain range, Sean's storytelling began to rile a flat-nosed ranch hand, who'd been losing most of the afternoon.

"If there's one thing I can't stand," Flat-nose said, as he got to his feet, "it's a Catholic. An' if I could stand a Catholic, I still couldn't stand an Irish Catholic. An' if I could stand an Irish Catholic, I'd still shoot ya between the eyes for bein' a cheat an' a card sharp."

Sean held up his hands, in an attempt to calm the situation. He may have been a reprobate, but he was never deliberately antagonistic.

"My friend . . ."

"I ain't your friend," Flat-nose said, cutting him off.

"I can't help bein' Catholic or bein' Irish," Sean continued in his friendly manner, "but if I was a card sharp, surely I would've won a lot more money, don't ya think?"

"That just makes ya a lousy card sharp," Flat-nose replied, which drew laughter from the crowd in the saloon.

Sean continued to try and talk his way out the confrontation. He even laughed along with the crowd at his own expense. "Maybe you're right, my friend. Maybe you're right."

"Shut up," Flat-nose said.

Every eye in the place was now focused on the two men, and no one appeared interested in stopping what might happen next. In fact, most were looking forward to it -- and placing bets on the outcome.

As Sean slowly rose to face his opponent, the other men at the table quickly moved out of any potential lines of fire.

Michael, who had been seated next to Flat-nose, hesitated long enough to remove his spectacles and slip them into his shirt pocket. Then he gathered his poker chips, as he slowly got to his feet -- and before anyone in the saloon knew what had happened -- Michael tossed his chips into the ranch hand's face and followed with a vicious left, knocking him to the floor.

Sean smiled, relieved he didn't have to try his hand at a quick draw, which he didn't want to do in the first place and wasn't very good at in the second.

Michael grabbed his left hand with his right. It felt like he might have broken a couple knuckles on Flat-nose's chin. He barely even noticed, when Sean called for him to "look out", before he was gang-rushed by two of Flat-nose's friends.

Sean cold-cocked one of the two men that had grabbed Michael from behind, only to be punched by Flat-nose, who had recovered from Michael's left. Sean fell back into the crowd, who seemed to be enjoying the fist fight even more than the possible gunplay. They tossed Sean back toward Flat-nose, who was ready for him, but not Michael, who had extricated himself from the ranch hand's friends and delivered another left across Flat-nose's nose.

As quickly as the crowd had moved back to be clear of any potential gunplay, they now moved in closer to get a better look at the punches and kicks, and, as they got too close, more and more of them got caught up in the bruising and bruises. After all, the only thing more fun than watching a good, old-fashioned saloon brawl was participating in it.

Fists, chairs, and whiskey bottles were thrown, as strangers punched strangers, and friends helped friends back up on their feet to continue in the fun.

The bartenders. card dealers, saloon girls and, especially, the owner of the saloon did their best to break up the brawl, before the crowd did too much damage to their place of business, but they were out-numbered and, ultimately, only added to the destruction.

With Flat-Nose and his two friends unconscious, Sean and Michael took advantage of the chaos to cash in their chips with the money in the cigar box on the poker table, which had served as the dealer's bank. Not sure how much they were due, since all the players' chips were scattered all over the floor, they decided to clean out the box, then put back a few dollars, so as not to seem too greedy or larcenous.

That done, they made their way toward the exit, doing their best to avoid eye contact with any of the brawlers. It seemed best to leave the fighting to those who appeared to enjoy it.

"I wish you'd learn to get along with people better, Seamus," Michael said in his northern Irish brogue.

"I get along with people fine, Michaleen," Sean said with a smile. "Some people just don't always get along with me."

Chapter Two

1845 -- Texas

"WRONG! Do it again!"

Michael Lonergan looked around at the other recruits to see what he was doing wrong.

"Don't look at them!" the sergeant bellowed. "Look at me!"

Michael had no idea what he had gotten himself into. The twenty-three year old refugee from the ravages of the Irish potato famine was fresh off the boat from Donegal, where he grew up speaking mostly Gaelic.

He found things even worse in the New World, if that was possible. Nativist Americans resented the large influx of poor, ignorant, Irish Catholics onto their shores and into their cities. The immigrants found work scarce and job signs often read, "No Irish Need Apply."

The United States Army, on the other hand, was looking to bolster their ranks, and recruiting officers were offering seven dollars a month, more than most Irish could make as civilians (when or if they could even find work), along with stories of glory and adventure and the possibility of fighting the English, the perennial, historical enemy of the Irish, over an ongoing dispute regarding the boundary line between Canada and the Oregon Territory, all of which appealed to the young Irishman, who, until he had talked to the recruiting officer, had not even thought of becoming a soldier.

Michael made his mark on a line at the bottom of the enlistment paper, not having the slightest idea what it said. He trusted the recruiting officer had been totally honest with him.

The officer neglected to mention the beatings or the brutality -- or that the dispute with England had been settled, but not the territorial dispute with Mexico.

"You're hopeless. Ignorant Irish papist." Sergeant Baxter shook his head. "How are we gonna beat the Mexican Army with a bunch of ignorant Irish papists?"

Sean Mulcahy resisted the temptation to give his new-found friend a sympathetic look. Even the slightest side glance, without so much as a turn of his head, while standing at attention, would only make the sergeant as angry at him as he was with Michael. And that wouldn't be of any help for either of them.

The platoon's lieutenant, a recent graduate from the Military Academy at West Point, watched the drilling of the recruits from his horse a short distance away and scowled.

"Tie him to a wagon wheel, sergeant, and give him thirty lashes. Maybe that will instill some sense of urgency into his drilling."

"Yes, sir!" The sergeant grinned through his usual snarl, then turned to his corporal. "You heard the lieutenant. It's thirty lashes for the stupid Mick!"

The corporal directed two soldiers to grab Michael by the shoulders and tie him to a large wagon wheel. Then the corporal ripped away the back of his shirt, while the platoon was ordered to face Michael to witness punishment.

Sergeant Baxter took his time uncoiling his six foot long, braided leather bullwhip, which he always kept close by, then cracked it a couple times, so the soldiers could hear the frightening sound the thing made.

The rawhide whip ripped into Michael's back like nothing he had ever felt before. He was struck mute with the first strike, then cried out after the second. Sergeant Baxter took a sadistic pride in his ability with the bullwhip, laying every stroke across a different part of the back, until the skin from the shoulders to the hips was laced with bloody streaks.

After the flogging, the barely conscious Private Lonergan was left tied to the wagon wheel, while the platoon returned to their drilling.

The newly christened American Army of Observation, under the command of General "Old Rough and Ready" Zachary Taylor, had been ordered by President James K. Polk to make camp at Kinney's Ranch, near Corpus Christi, Texas. War with Mexico was imminent, if the War Hawks in Congress had their way, and the Army of Observation was there, waiting to move south, when the order arrived from the War Office in Washington.

Kinney's Ranch proved to be a poor location for the army to bivouac in November and December of 1845. Extreme heat wore down the recruits during the day, while blistering cold and freezing rain at night caused the exhausted soldiers to nearly freeze to death in the thread-worn excuse for two-man tents the War Office had supplied them. Pneumonia and dysentery ran rampant through the camp that winter, and a great many died.

The west country Irishmen fared better than most. They were used to drastic weather, living along the coast of the cold, cruel North Atlantic. Michael Lonergan had grown up fishing in the rough seas in animal-skin currachs off the coast of Donegal. Young Patrick Kelly came from a family of farmers in County Sligo, while big, tough Jamie Murphy grew up on the rocky coast of Galway, until he ran away to join the British Army, and good-natured Sean Mulcahy grew up in the city of Cork, down the road from Blarney Castle, close enough for it to rub off on him.

For those not on sick call, drilling and discipline were the orders of the day, and the eager young West Point graduates that made up the junior officer corps were anxious to prove which of them was the most aggressive disciplinarian in the army.

This made life all the rougher for the Irish immigrant recruits, who bore the brunt of most of the disciplinary action. If an example was needed to put the fear of God into a platoon, an Irish Catholic was singled out, usually receiving twice the amount of punishment a native-born Protestant recruit might be given for the same offense.

And Michael Lonergan was made to order. He was far from being a natural soldier, which Sergeant Baxter quickly observed. He slouched in formation, until the sergeant reminded him at the top of his lungs to stand at attention. And he was always about a half second behind the others, when it came to the manual of arms, mostly because he was left-handed and his English was so poor.

When Baxter finally dismissed the recruits from the day's drilling, Private Sean Mulcahy approached the sergeant.

"Request permission to release Private Lonergan," Sean said respectfully. "I'm sure he's learned his lesson."

The sergeant glared at Michael. "I guess so. He's a sorry excuse for a soldier, but the army needs cannon fodder."

Sean and Jamie Murphy carefully untied their friend from the wagon wheel, while Patrick Kelly gave him a sip of water from his canteen.

"There now, boyo. Don't drink too much."

"I don't think I can stand," Michael said in his native Gaelic.

"Now now, Michael," Jamie told him. "Ya can't let the bastards think they broke ya."

"Won't do a t'all," Sean said.

"Bad for all of us," Patrick added.

"Especially for Patrick, here. If they break ya, the sergeant'll have to start makin' an example o' Paddy," Jamie said, reminding Patrick he wasn't much better at soldiering than Michael.

Sean massaged his friend's legs to bring back some circulation.

"He's gonna do this to me again, tomorrow," Michael said. "That damned sergeant hates me."

"He just doesn't like the way ya do the manual of arms," Jamie told him. "Ya gotta put some snap into it. That's the way I learned it in the British army."

"I can't understand what he's sayin' half the time," Michael complained. "It's like he's spittin' out gibberish."

"Come on," Sean said. "Let's get ya cleaned up quick, or we'll miss mess call. Then ya can get a good night's sleep."

"That won't be hard," Michael muttered.

Chapter Three

October 30, 1879 -- California

Several days after the saloon fight, Sean and Michael made camp in a quiet nest of trees near the Diablo Range. They were heading for the Pacific coast; its mild winters seemed more inviting to them than the deep snow and frozen cold of the Sierra Nevada mountains.

Both of them were tired and chilled to the bone, so they made their campfire a little larger than they might have otherwise. They knew that the larger the fire, the greater the chance it might draw strangers -- and not always the friendly kind. But the warmth of the flames made the hard ground on that cold October night feel just a little more tolerable.

"I think we should spend the whole winter in one place, somewhere along the coast," Michael said.

"In one place?"

"Sure. Why not?"

"Well, for one thing," Sean said, "travelin's what we do best."

"Travel's great, when you're young -- but awful painful on the joints as ya get older."

Sean massaged his arthritic left hip, the result of a bullet he took years ago.

"I suppose ya got a point," Sean conceded. "Though I don't know what either of us'd do, settled in one place for any length o' time. We've been many things, Michaleen: good soldiers, bad farmers, worse prospectors, competent laborers on the railroad, better gamblers than most, an', occasionally, fake Franciscan friars. Now, we're too old to be soldiers, farmers, prospectors, or laborers on the railroad. That leaves gamblers an' bein' fake Franciscan friars, an' neither of those are appropriate professions for anyone thinkin' of remainin' in one place for any length o' time."

"Maybe we need to find a new profession."

"Let's face it," Sean said. "Neither of us figured we'd live this long. Otherwise, we'd have married an' had children to support us in our old age."

Michael sighed as he smiled, agreeing with his friend, but with an air of resolved melancholy.

Sean tried to brighten his friend's mood by composing a poem off the top of his head, as he had many times before:

"My good friend, you an' me, it must be destiny,
How we've survived to this day an' the next.
Whether bright or black, we've had each other's back,"

Sean paused, causing Michael to wonder, if his friend was stuck for a last line. Then Sean smiled and finished with:

"An' kept the winds o' fate forever vexed"

Michael laughed. "I thought ya'd boxed yourself into a corner, comin' up with a rhyme for 'next,'"

"Only for a moment, Michaleen. Only for a moment."

Michael pulled a bottle of Irish whiskey from his saddlebag and offered it to Sean, who took a long swig, before passing it back.

"Then again," Sean added, as an afterthought. "I wouldn't be adverse to tradin' my horse an' saddle for a cushioned seat on a train or my bedroll for a soft down bed in a fine hotel now an' again. I know my hip would approve."

"What you need is a rich widow who could provide ya with those cushioned seats an' soft down beds."

Sean smiled. "From your lips to God's ears, Michaleen. An', hopefully, she wouldn't be adverse to a bit o' travelin'."

"First class, of course."

"Of course."

They were cleaning up after dinner, when they first heard the sound of human feet and horse hooves approaching in the dark.

"Sounds like two comin' from the south," Michael whispered.

Sean nodded. "An' at least two more from the north."

They both lifted the small leather loops off the hammers of their revolvers that kept the guns secure in their holsters, then Michael reached into his saddlebag on the ground beside him and pulled out something that he hid under his leg.

"You in the camp," a voice called out from the dark. "We're comin' in."

Michael took off his spectacles and wiped away the smudges. "How's your stomach, Seamus?"

Sean smiled.

Michael returned the spectacles to his face, as two large, grizzled-looking men walked slowly into the light from the south, leading their ponies with their left hands, while their right hands were close enough to their holstered guns to infer their intentions.

A balding man with a scar over his right eye stepped forward. "Any coffee left?"

"Help yourself," Michael replied in his northern Irish brogue. "There should be enough left for you an' your friend, an' your two friends behind us."

The balding fellow smiled, and called out, "Come on in, boys."

Two more men who clearly hadn't seen a bathtub or razor blade in months, ambled into the light from the campfire, also holding the reins to their ponies with their left hands. They had already drawn their pistols and were pointing them at the two Irishmen.

The balding fellow crouched down and took hold of the coffee pot with his gloved hand to pour himself a cup. Almost immediately, he spit it back out.

"It's burnt," he said. "And weak!"

"Sorry."

"We didn't really come for the coffee anyway," the balding fellow said, as he got back to his feet. Then he motioned for the second, younger fellow who had come in with him from the south to step forward.

While the two men from the north kept their guns at the ready, the younger fellow squatted down in front of Michael and proceeded to strip him of everything he had in his pockets, whether it had any value or not. Lastly, he took Michael's revolver.

"A Colt," he said, happily, and slipped it under his belt.

Sean had remained uncharacteristically silent. He just sat on his bedroll with a sullen look on his face. Suddenly, he winced in pain and doubled over, holding his stomach.

15

"What's wrong with him?" the balding fellow asked.

"Stomach pains," Michael said. "We're on our way to the nearest town to see a doctor about it."

The younger fellow reached down and grabbed Sean by the shoulders in order to sit him back up -- just what the Irishman wanted him to do.

Sean pulled Michael's Colt from the younger robber's belt and shot a hole clean through his midsection.

This surprised the others just long enough for Michael to draw a second gun he had hidden under his leg, then twist his body and blast away, hitting the two men behind him square in their chests, before turning back around to point his revolver at the only one not yet bleeding. He didn't need to keep looking at the robbers behind him, but their leader watched, as the two men gasped one last breath each, then crumbled to the ground, dead before they hit it.

Michael and the balding robber stared at one another for a moment, waiting for the other to make a move -- until Sean shot the man in the temple.

"He made fun o' your coffee," Sean said, as he pushed the younger man off of him.

The two Irishmen laid out the four dead robbers side-by-side, then Michael retrieved his recently lost possessions from the younger man, before joining Sean in searching the pockets of the others for anything of value: money, gold, jewelry, and, of course, guns and ammunition. They found quite a lot. Apparently, the dead men had been successful thieves.

Afterward, they checked the ponies for what might be in the saddlebags: a couple extra shirts, some food, jerky, coffee, and, surprisingly, some reasonably fresh, if slightly bruised, fruit.

"Oranges for breakfast, Sean!" Michael declared.

Sean found a Winchester repeating rifle cradled in a saddle sling on one of the horses. "Been thinkin' o' buyin' one o' these."

They took the saddles and blankets off the ponies and led them to a patch of grass, where their horses had been grazing, then removed their bridles, so they could eat as well, while tethered with ropes tied to trees to keep them from wandering away. Then, they brushed their matted, dirty coats, something the robbers clearly hadn't done in quite some time.

The ponies all had brands, which meant they were probably stolen, which meant it would be dangerous for the Irishmen to keep them. The last thing they needed was to be caught with stolen ponies, even if they hadn't been the ones who stole them. Horse stealing was a hanging offense, and they were strangers in these parts, with no one to vouch for their innocence. But neither of them wanted to just set the ponies free up on the cold, desolate mountain range.

As for the robbers, Sean and Michael had thought for a moment about taking them to the nearest town to collect any reward there might be on them, but without any wanted posters, let alone even knowing who they were, they might not be able to prove the robbers were, in fact, robbers.

"Besides," as Michael said, "we may be gamblers and fake Franciscans, but we aren't bounty hunters."

So, the two men buried the robbers in shallow graves, without any markers. Still, Sean felt compelled to say a prayer over them. Father Seamus was never far from his consciousness.

The next morning, they headed out at first light, keeping an eye out for anyone who might happen to see them with the stolen ponies.

After an hour or so in the saddle, they came out of a cluster of trees to see a truly beautiful sight: a herd of wild mustangs racing across the valley in the distance, running free and defiant.

The ponies saw them, too, and began to whinny and stamp their feet.

The two men dismounted from their horses and removed the bridles once again from the branded ponies.

"Go on, then," Sean said, just above a whisper. "Have a run with your new friends."

Michael and Sean barely had to encourage the ponies with a couple swats on their hind quarters, before they took off at the gallop toward the mustang herd.

The two Irishmen watched them and smiled.

Then, Sean was inspired to add, as he took notice of the lead mustang out front:

"What a sight to see, runnin' wild an' free,
Kickin' up his heels . . ."

"They're hooves, not heels," Michael added, finishing the line.

"Across the broad terrain," Sean continued, undeterred,
"Wind flowin' through his mane.
Aye, me an' Michaleen knows how that feels."

Michael laughed, once again amazed at how his traveling companion could master his rhyme and meter on the spur of the moment.

Sean just continued to watch the ponies run joyfully with the herd of mustangs -- until they disappeared from view over a ridge in the distance.

Chapter Four

1846 -- Texas

In the spring of 1846, General Zachary Taylor received orders from the Secretary of War to move the Army of Observation south from Kinney's Ranch to the northern bank of the Rio Grande River, territory claimed by both Texas and Mexico. Taylor also changed the name of his command to the Army of Occupation, in anticipation of their next move.

Once they got to the Rio Grande, the junior officers quickly returned to their brutal treatment of the Catholic immigrants.

Gunther, a German Catholic in Sean and Michael's company, caught the wrath of their incensed captain, who had him branded on the forehead with the letters "HD" for habitual drunkard, while Daniel, an Irish recruit, was ordered to ride the horse for the most trivial of offense.

Seated on top of a high, wooden sawhorse, Daniel had his hands tied behind his back and iron weights tied to his ankles. After four hours of this torture, he passed out and fell to the ground. When the soldiers guarding him went to put him back on the sawhorse, they discovered his neck had been broken from the fall.

Another Irishman, named Colin, who usually stood next to Sean in assembly, had his head laid open, when their lieutenant struck him with the flat side of his saber. He died of his wounds the next day.

A few days later, leaflets began circulating through the camp, encouraging the Catholic recruits to desert and join the Catholic Mexican Army. They were promised better treatment, better food, instant Mexican citizenship, and two hundred acres of land they could farm after the war.

How and when the Mexicans had learned of the double standard in military discipline issued out by Protestant officers on Catholic soldiers, no one was sure, but it had an immediate effect. Catholic immigrant recruits began swimming across the Rio Grande almost every night, so much so, Catholics were not allowed to be on picket duty, for fear they wouldn't shoot at any deserters in the water -- or they might even desert themselves.

Sean, Michael, Jamie, and Patrick knew of the flyers. Sean had even read one of them to Michael and Patrick.

It sounded too good to be true. But it meant breaking the oath they took, when they joined the United States Army.

"We're not even American citizens," Patrick argued. "Just hired mercenaries, fightin' for 'em."

"These Protestant officers treat us like dirt," Sean said. "Just ask Colin, Daniel, or Gunther."

"I was better treated in the British Army," Jamie said, "an' their officers are narrow-minded, inbred sons-o'-bitches."

Michael found himself temporarily spared from their lieutenant's wrath.

As the days passed, and Michael began to recover from the whipping at Kinney's Ranch, he felt more like playing his fiddle after evening mess. He didn't play it with any great precision or had much of a repertory, but he had a natural feel for running the bow across the strings, and the other men enjoyed listening.

Michael's company commander, an ambitious captain anxious for promotion, happened to hear him play one evening and decided he might score some points by having the Irishman play for the senior officers' mess.

"I want you to start off with something by Mozart," the captain told him. "That's a favorite of the general's."

"I don't know who that is, sir."

"Of course you don't, you ignorant Mick. How about 'Yankee Doodle'? You know 'Yankee Doodle'?"

"Yankee who?"

"God. What was I thinking? And I suppose, if I got some sheet music from one of the other musicians in the camp, you couldn't read that, either."

"I can't even read English."

The captain growled his disgust. "Just play a couple of those papist-Irish songs I heard you play the other night."

"Yes, sir. I'll do me best."

"You damn well better. Or it's the lash for you again, you dirty Mick."

With his favorite whipping boy now off limits from punishment, the frustrated lieutenant ordered Sergeant Baxter to focus his attention on Patrick, Sean, and Jamie: Patrick, because he was the second worst at the manual of arms, Sean, because he was Lonergan's best friend and tent mate, and Jamie, because he had committed the unpardonable offense of

21

lifting his eyebrow in contempt during one of the lieutenant's numerous confused commands.

Sean and Jamie were buck and gagged. Soldiers forced them to sit on the ground, pushing their knees up into their chests and binding their wrists in front of their shins. Then poles were shoved under their bent knees and above their arms, and a gag was stuffed in their mouths to keep them from crying out in pain.

Patrick was sentenced to a flogging, like Michael had been, except the lieutenant had ordered fifty lashes for Patrick's failure at the manual of arms.

Sean and Jamie watched from their excruciating positions, as Sergeant Baxter laid on his whip, ripping Patrick apart, physically, mentally, and emotionally. He was unconscious after twenty strokes, so the corporal revived him with a bucket of cold water thrown on him.

Michael gave his concert, which went over well with the officers, then made a quick retreat and headed back toward the rows of small, two-man tents.

On the way, he came across Jamie and Sean, still buck and gagged on the ground, and Patrick, tied to the wagon wheel.

"Jesus, Mary, and Joseph," Michael cried out, in a loud whisper.

He ran over to his friends and immediately started to cut them from their bindings, starting with Sean.

"How can anyone treat someone like this?" Michael said in his native Gaelic, then added in English, "It's inhuman."

"The sergeant didn't have you to pick on, so he took his bile out on us," Sean said, rubbing his legs.

Michael cut Jamie loose next, then rushed over to Patrick.

"He's been out for some time," Jamie called out.

Michael held Patrick's head up. "Paddy. It's me, Michael. Wake up."

But Patrick Kelly was dead.

"Holy Mother of God," Jamie cried out. "In all my years o' servin' in the British Army, I never saw anything like this. At the rate they're goin', there won't be any of us left for the Mexicans to kill!"

"Well, I'm not waitin'," Sean said, as he looked over at Patrick, still tied to the wheel. "I'm swimmin' across tonight."

Jamie nodded in agreement.

Michael helped his two friends to the edge of the Rio Grande, then waited with them, until the soldiers on picket were the furthest away.

Michael looked at Sean and Jamie. Their legs, arms, backs, and shoulders were racked with pain from being trussed up in that unconscionable position.

"You two'll never make it on your own. I'll have to pull ya across."

Michael looked at his fiddle one last time, then tossed it in the bushes. He would need both arms to help his friends.

Chapter Five

October 31, 1879 -- California

Shushu's future appeared as bleak as her past. The little girl had been born in a poor village a few days journey outside of Canton. Her father had worked, when he could find work, as a laborer, to supplement what little they earned from their meager farm.

Then, when she was seven years old, her father sold Shushu to the Zhang family. Master Zhang had received an offer to come to America to work for his cousin, Master Lau, who had a successful general store in the Chinatown district of Monterey, California, and wanted to open a second shop in the Chinese fishing village just outside of town at Point Alones.

The Zhangs decided they should bring a future bride for their ten year old son, Ping. They had been told in the letter from Master Lau that Chinese girls were in short supply in America, and anti-immigration laws were making it even more difficult for them to come over.

Shushu didn't want to go. She didn't like the Zhangs. She hated the voyage across the Pacific, even more so since Ping kept threatening to toss her overboard. And she didn't like her life in the new country. She was nothing more than a servant, relegated to any menial chore a seven year old was capable of, and some she wasn't, but was told to do anyway. Madame Zhang demanded obedience from the occasionally willful child and beat her regularly, whether or not she deserved it. Then Ping would tease her to make her angry, which caused Madame Zhang to beat her all the more.

She tried to make friends with the Chinese fishermen's daughters, but Madame Zhang gave her little time to play.

Her eighth birthday came and went without the slightest acknowledgment.

The last Friday of every month, Master Zhang would close the store early and take his family for a picnic on the sand dunes south of Point Alones. They enjoyed the sea air and would walk barefoot up and down the dunes.

Poor Shushu always fell behind. She just couldn't keep up with the others, and they couldn't be bothered to slow down or wait for her. It didn't help that she was made to carry the wicker food basket for them.

On one Friday excursion on an overcast autumn afternoon, Shushu had fallen so far behind that she lost sight of the Zhangs over a sand dune. She was feeling particularly willful that day and grumbled to herself, as she trudged up the tall dune against the shifting sand.

Suddenly, she heard a commotion, yelling in Chinese and in English, followed by popping sounds and cries for help.

By the time she could look over the summit of the dune, the commotion had ceased. The three Zhangs were lying in the sand, while two young white men stood over them, laughing. One of them, wearing a brown hat, leaned over and searched Master Zhang's pockets for whatever he could find, while a second one, in a black hat, took Madame Zhang's jade necklace from around her neck. A third young man, in a grey hat, held onto their horses on a grassy stretch off the edge of the sand. Once they finished with the Zhangs, the men got on their horses and rode off toward Monterey.

Shushu waited for quite some time -- until the young men had long disappeared into the distance -- before she ventured down the other side of the dune and walked over to the Zhangs.

They were dead. The little girl had seen dead people back in China. She attended her beloved grandfather's funeral, when he was laid out with his *ehru*, the musical instrument he played so beautifully, beside him.

She didn't know what to do. She didn't like the Zhangs, but they were the only people she knew in America, except for the Laus, and she liked them even less. Master Lau would probably just sell her, like her father had done. The Laus didn't have a son looking for a Chinese girl to marry some day.

So, the little girl sat in the sand several feet from the Zhangs and looked out at the crashing waves of the Pacific Ocean which separated her from China.

Sean and Michael made good time, as they headed west. They wanted to put as much space between them and the scene of the shootout as possible.

Neither of them liked gunplay, but they had become good at it, especially Michael, who was as quick on the draw as anyone he'd come across -- so far. Sean wasn't as quick, but his aim, more often than not, was just as accurate.

As they grew closer to the ocean, the smell of salt sea air reminded them of their youths back in Ireland, especially Michael.

"By the way," Sean said to his friend. "It just occurred to me. Tonight's All Hallows' Eve."

"So i' tis," Michael replied. "Samhain. The Celtic New Year."

"When the veil between this world an' the other can be drawn back, if the brave or the curious are so inclined," Sean said, remembering something he had learned long ago as a boy. "Or something like that."

Michael looked over at his friend. "Have ya ever tried to draw back the veil?"

"No. I don't think I believe in all that."

"That's probably why you're better at sayin' Mass than I am."

Sean smiled.

As the two men passed along the edge of the coastline, they came across three bodies lying in the sand, and a little girl staring out at the ocean.

Shushu noticed the white men approach. They didn't look like the other men, exactly -- and there were only two of them -- but she'd had no other contact with white men before. Perhaps all white men hated the Chinese.

When Sean and Michael got to the edge of the sand, they dismounted and walked over to the three bodies.

They were clearly Chinese, probably recent immigrants, based on the traditional Chinese clothing they were wearing, unlike some of the Chinese miners and laborers they had met in their travels who had been in America long enough to learn some English and adopt more American-style clothing.

Michael examined the adult male. He had been struck in the head and shot in the back, probably while he was lying in the sand. The adult female and male child also had obvious bullet wounds.

Sean looked over at the little girl. "Is this your family?"

He couldn't tell if she understood him or not, though he suspected she didn't. He decided to approach her, then stopped when she began to back away.

"It's okay," Sean said with his warm, engaging smile. "I'm not gonna hurt ya."

The little girl didn't appear to be injured in any way. Sean tried to get closer to make sure, but she kept scooting away from him.

"I promise I won't hurt ya," he repeated.

She didn't appear to believe him.

"Have ya been here long?" he asked. "Are ya hungry? Thirsty?"

Shushu continued to cringe silently, well out of his reach.

Sean took his water canteen off his shoulder and offered it to her. She didn't seem to recognize what it was, so he took a drink himself, then offered it to her once again. Shushu slowly got to her feet and even more slowly crossed in closer. Sean held out the canteen as far as his arm could reach.

Finally, she came close enough to take hold of it. She held it over her head to take a drink, but wound up spilling some of the water on herself.

"Well, that's one way to do it, I suppose," Sean said.

The Irishman took back the canteen, then looked in the wicker basket sitting not far from her and found a cup.

"Let's try that again," he said.

Shushu took the cup and drank down the water, pretty much in one gulp.

"Thirsty, eh? Here's some more."

Sean refilled the cup, as Michael crossed over to join them.

"She hurt in any way?"

"Doesn't appear to be."

Michael crouched down to get a better look at her. "Why didn't they shoot the girl?"

"Don't know."

"Maybe she's not real," Michael said. "Maybe she's a faerie, a Chinese sprite -- an' made herself invisible to protect herself."

Michael smiled at the little girl, hoping to evoke a smile in return, but she just stared back at him.

"I suppose we should bury the others an' take the girl to Monterey," Sean said. "Leave her with the town marshal."

"Should we take the basket of food?" Michael asked.

"I don't see why not," Sean replied. "I'm sure the little girl is hungry."

Michael picked up the basket. "I know I am."

Shushu had never been on a horse before, and she wasn't sure she liked the idea, when Sean picked her up and set her down on the saddle of the large animal, before he climbed up behind her and placed her tiny hands on the saddle's horn.

"Hold on, little one," Sean said, then patted her head, before grabbing the reins and giving his horse a kick.

As the trio continued north, they came across what looked like the ruins of a church in the twilight, beside a quiet river, a once impressive stone structure, with asymmetrical

29

bell towers situated on either side of the entrance, and a Moorish dome set upon the left tower. Beside the church, sat the rubbled remains of other structures, made of dried mud bricks that had been reduced to a muddy mess due to the winds and rains over the years.

"Begorah," Michael said, just above a whisper.

"This must be one of those California missions that were strung up an' down the coastline," Sean said.

"Looks abandoned."

"Let's have a look." Sean had always been the more adventuresome of the two. "Perhaps we can spend the night in there."

The basilica was in a state of complete disrepair. Several of the heavy wooden beams that had once held up the ceiling had long since fallen to the floor or were lying on top of the wooden pews.

"So much for sleepin' under a ceilin' tonight," Michael said, with a sigh.

Undeterred, Sean decided he wanted to explore the place further.

As he walked through the mission building, Sean saw that most of the sacred ornamentation that had decorated the sanctuary had long since been removed, although some of the carved woodwork still remained around the pulpit, and a couple of the wall frescoes could still be made out, like faded shadows looking down on him. It was both eerie and intriguing at the same time.

Finally, Michael heard his friend call out from the back of the basilica.

"Michaleen! Back here. The sacristy has a roof."

"How old is it?" Michael called back. "Will it fall in on us in the middle of the night?"

"No. It looks like it's been recently built. An' it's plenty big enough for all three of us."

Michael looked over at Shushu. "What d'ya think? Is it sacrilegious to sleep in a sacristy?"

The little girl had no idea what he was talking about.

Michael clutched the reins of both horses in one hand, then held out his other for her to take hold of. But the little girl hesitated. The long, dark, scary shadows that spread across the former church caused by the setting sun filled the little girl with a feeling of foreboding, almost as if she could sense the ghosts of the ruins making an appearance.

"Maybe you're right," Michael said. "Might be better to walk around on the outside -- so whatever's left of the ceiling doesn't come down on us."

As Michael escorted Shushu along the north side of the building, they looked out at the setting sun and the orange glow of twilight. It was beautiful.

"Happy Samhain, little sprite," Michael said. "Happy Samhain."

Chapter Six

1846 -- Mexico

Sean, Michael, and Jamie rested on the south side of the Rio Grande, behind the cover of trees, so some smart-aleck sharpshooter working the picket line across the river couldn't make a name for himself by picking off the three deserters.

After a few minutes to catch their breath, which was about all they could risk, the three Irishmen made their way in the direction of the main Mexican army camp. All the American soldiers knew where it was. The scouts had located it, and the camp rumor mill had spread the word. It was just out of reach of the American cannons across the river.

They were captured by Mexican pickets and found themselves standing before a smartly dressed officer, who spoke just enough English to interrogate them.

"What are your names?"

"James Murphy."

"Sean Mulcahy."

"Michael Lonergan."

"Why are you here?"

"We read your leaflet," Sean said. "Said you were recruitin' Catholic soldiers."

"You are deserters?"

"Well, the way we figure it," Jamie said, "we weren't really American citizens, so we weren't really American soldiers. More like mercenaries."

"If you join the Mexican Army, you will immediately become Mexican citizens," the officer told them. "And there will be no deserting back to the American Army."

"I doubt they'd take us back," Sean replied. "Probably just hang us and be done with us."

"No," Jamie said. "The American Army shoots deserters."

"It is the same with the Mexican Army."

The three Irishmen traded in their soggy, light blue fatigue jackets and trousers for the dashing dark blue uniforms of the Mexican infantry that would not look out of place on any European military parade ground.

They were assigned to the *Legión de Extranjeros,* the Mexican Foreign Legion, an infantry unit made up almost exclusively of deserters from the American Army, but with Mexican officers.

Life was not much different from that in the American camp: drilling, drilling, and more drilling, except that they had an Irish-born drill instructor, Tommy Muldoon, who, like Jamie, was a veteran of the British Army. He was harsh and firm on discipline, but practical, instead of vicious, when it came to punishment.

The first element of their training involved learning how to use the twenty year-old British surplus Brown Bess flintlocks with any sort of accuracy at long range. Michael was never much good with a long barreled weapon, but Sean and Jamie got the hang of firing the flintlock from the hip as the Mexicans did, since they used more gunpowder in their charges than the British, and firing the Brown Bess with the extra powder from the shoulder could easily dislocate it.

Unlike the nativists American soldiers, the Mexicans welcomed their new *compañeros de armes* and did their best to help them acclimate to life south of the border.

Sean quickly took it upon himself to learn almost enough Spanish to converse, but one aspect of the new army that took some time to adjust to was the Mexican cuisine. The Irish were used to a milder diet and did not have much experience with the hot spices, which the Mexicans regularly added to their enchiladas, tamales, and tortillas.

Jamie and Michael tried to limit their meals to whatever had the least amount of spice, but Sean was always eager to try new things.

One day, the three Irishmen observed a couple of Mexican infantrymen eating small red vegetables from a bowl.

"What are those?" Sean asked in his ever-increasing Spanish.

"Chile peppers," a bearded corporal told him.

"You eat 'em plain?"

"If you are able," another soldier said.

"That sounds like a challenge."

Sean sat with the others and picked up one of the red chiles, then looked up at Michael and Jamie, before taking a bite.

He had never tasted anything like it before. It was like his mouth was on fire.

"Bloody bleedin' hell!" Sean said, then panted, repeatedly.

The Mexican soldiers broke out in laughter, then handed him glass after glass of water to extinguish the fire.

"You've got guts," the corporal said in his heavily accented English.

"You speak English?"

"A little. There are more and more Yanquis moving into my hometown of Monterey."

The corporal held out his hand. "Roberto Fuentes."

Sean and Roberto shook hands, then the corporal handed the Irishman a bottle of tequila to wash away the remaining sting in his mouth.

On May 13, 1846, the American Government declared war on Mexico. The Mexican Government had already declared a defensive war against the United States on April 23rd and followed up with a full declaration of war on July 7th.

The first engagements did not go well for the Mexican Army, and they were forced to fall back from the border, allowing Taylor's Army of Occupation to cross the Rio Grande.

Meanwhile, word spread that an artillery battalion was being formed, made up mostly of Irish deserters with any cannon experience. It was to be named the San Patricios, after the Irish patron saint, and would be led by another Irish deserter, who had also been a veteran of the British Army, Lieutenant John Riley.

Jamie was one of the first transferred to the unit and was quickly promoted to sergeant.

More hands-on than most of the American junior officers, Lieutenant Riley insisted on conducting morning inspection, personally.

Afterwards, Sergeant Murphy dismissed the troops for breakfast, then requested a word with Riley.

"I'd like you to consider adding Sean Mulcahy and Michael Lonergan to our battalion, Sir."

"Are they artillery men?" Riley asked.

"They're quick learners," Jamie said, "An' I'll vouch for their characters."

Right off, Sean and Michael took to being gunners, even as they were assigned every menial job, like polishing the brass cannons and caring for the horses that were used to haul the big guns and the limbers, the wagons that carried some of the gunpowder and projectiles. Later, under Riley's supervision, they learned how to uncouple the cannons from the limbers, wheel them into position, and load and prime the guns in a matter of minutes.

Most of all, they enjoyed the camaraderie of being in a battalion made up primarily of other Irishmen.

The only thing they didn't particularly like was how loud the cannons got, when they were fired.

"How do gunners keep from goin' deaf?" Sean asked Jamie at one point.

"What?" Jamie answered back.

Sean hoped he was joking.

To pass the time during the long evenings after dinner call, many of the San Patricios swapped tales, telling some of the English-speaking Mexicans of all the different roundabout paths each of them had made on their way to Mexico. Some had come via Boston or New York or Charleston, South Carolina. Many had served in the British Army or Navy, before mustering out or deserting in Canada or the West

Indies, while a couple of the older soldiers had served in Napoleon's Irish Legion and fought against the English, before emigrating to New Orleans after Waterloo.

At one point, a Mexican soldier whose English was almost as good as Roberto Fuentes' wondered, "Why do so many Irish leave their country?"

"Well," Sean replied, with an ironic smile, "i' tis a long story, but it goes something like this:

> As the north wind blows, so the story goes,
> The Irish never planned to leave their home.
> Then England set 'em straight,
> Told 'em, 'Travelin' was great!'
> An' set the Gaels a-startin' for to roam."

Not all the Mexicans picked up on Sean's Celtic mischievous irony in the poem, but it was obvious to the Irish, who smiled throughout the telling of the sad tale Sean had been working on for quite some time, first in the U.S. camp, and then in Mexico.

> "The story then goes on, so many Gaels had gone,
> For English rule encouraged Irish flight.
> The Ulster Earls to Spain, Wild Geese to Aquitaine,
> Where e'er they went, the Irish found a fight.

> "And as their hist'ry shows, and so their legend grows,
> North winds conspired to keep their sails unfurled.
> West Indies to Westphalia, an' far away Australia,
> The Gaels, they rode the winds all 'round the world.

> "Whence the legend grows, an' fables, they disclose,
> No matter where the Irish folk have been.
> By choice or deportation, wherever their destination,
> The Irish have survived, time an' again.

"The fables, they disclose, and chronicles expose
For in the time of Erin's great despair:
Blight, *an Gorta Mór*, drove thousands from our shore,
An' finally to America's dubious care.

"So the chronicles unfold, and the sordid tale is told,
How 'merica ne'er succumbed to Gaelic charms.
For us, they had no use, an' heaped on us abuse,
While Mexico welcomed us with open arms."

Even the Mexican soldiers who didn't speak much,
if any, English found Sean's lively poem entrancing and
applauded along with the Irish, who could readily identify
with it.

By September, the Mexican Army of the North, under
the command of General Pedro de Ampudia, had established
fortifications in and around the city of Monterrey and waited
for the Americans to march south.

The San Patricios set up their cannons in an imposing
citadel, directly in the path of the American troops. This
would be their baptism of fire as an artillery battalion, and
each man was anxious to prove himself, no one more so than
Sean and Michael.

While they were with the *Legión de Extranjeros*, they
had been held in reserve. Now, at Monterrey, they were right
in the front line.

Two companies of infantry were assigned to the citadel
as support for the Irish cannoneers, and Sean found himself
next to Corporal Fuentes, who was with the *Batallón de
Independencia.*

"Protectin' your hometown, eh Bob?" Sean said.

Fuentes shook his head. "Wrong Monterrey, amigo. I'm
from the Monterey in Alta California. And it's Roberto, not
Bob. We're in Mexico, not America."

Sean nodded. "Fair enough, Bob."

Sean and Michael loaded the gunpowder and projectiles in cannon number four, then Jamie double-checked its elevation and pulled the lanyard. Grape shot and canister cut into the American lines, while Sean and Michael became blackened by the repeated blasts and deafened by the roar. They may have been afraid, but they didn't panic and didn't run. They did their duty.

Many of the San Patricios kept a running commentary on how the battle was progressing, which kept up their morale, even as members of the battalion were injured or killed by return fire. Jamie described it as the bravado of battle. Sean preferred to call it the 'blarney' of battle.

The San Patricios fired their cannons with lethal accuracy, cutting into the American advance with grape and canister, exacting a bloody toll, driving the Americans back, and winning the day.

Celebration was in order, but it was short-lived. Two days later, after a rain storm temporarily suspended the fighting, General Taylor changed tactics and attacked the Mexican flanks, forcing General Ampudia to concede, seek a truce, and withdraw his troops to the south, through the Mexican desert.

The terrain was alien to the Irishmen, with its coarse brush, all the different varieties of spiky cacti, nasty-looking creatures, and most of all, way too many snakes, which Sean and Michael were particularly afraid of.

"Bloody bleedin' hell!" Sean called out at one point. "Do ya think, when St. Patrick drove all the snakes from Ireland, they all came to Mexico?"

"What's the matter, Sean?" Roberto asked, with a laugh. "Don't ya like snakes?"

"What's to like?" he replied. "They're slimy and slippery, and some make that rattlin' noise."

"Be glad they do," Roberto told him. "The ones that rattle are the ones you need to stay away from."

"I'd as soon stay away from all of 'em," Michael said.

"Shneaky shnaaakes," Sean added, in an exaggerated drawling brogue, then explained to the Mexicans, "It's an expression we have back in County Cork, for anything or anyone who's sneaky, slithery, or sly."

The San Patricios regrouped in San Luis Potosi, where Michael found a used and well-worn fiddle in a shop and began to play it straight away.

"You're not much of a talker, Michael, like Sean there," Roberto said, pointing at Mulcahy, "but you play a good fiddle."

Michael smiled. "That's because I'm from the northern part of Erin, an' Sean's from the south."

"What's that got to do with it?"

"Ya see," Sean told him, "long ago, there were these two great warrior brothers who conquered Ireland, then proceeded to divide up the population between themselves, each taking an equal number of warriors, artists, an' artisans, until all that remained were one last poet an' one last harper. So, the two great warrior brothers drew lots, an' the harpist went to the brother in the north, an' the poet went to the brother in the south. An' that is why, to this day, the northern part of Erin is known for its musicians, an' the south is known for its poets."

Michael played another tune, this one a lively air, which drew a good sized crowd of appreciative listeners.

Soon enough, the Mexican soldiers began to call the quiet, black Irishman "Miguelito", while the Irish called him "Michaleen".

Soon after their arrival in San Luis Potosi, the Mexican Army stood at full attention to greet the newly re-installed president and commander-in-chief of Mexico, Antonio López de Santa Anna, recently returned from his exile in Cuba, where he had been forced to go after his humiliating defeat at San Jacinto during the Texas Revolution.

Santa Anna had been so impressed with their effectiveness at Monterrey, he issued the San Patricios with the Mexican Army's heaviest cannons, which they would put to brutal use in subsequent battles.

They were also greeted with a new banner, brand new battalion colors that had been designed by Lieutenant John Riley and sewn by the nuns in a nearby convent: a flag of green silk, with a golden Irish harp set below the Mexican Coat of Arms. Under the Coat of Arms were the words, *Liberatad por la Republica Mexicana* (Liberty for the Mexican Republic), while directly under the harp was the Gaelic expression, *Erin go Bragh* (Ireland Forever).

It was a flag worth fighting for, and possibly dying under.

Chapter Seven

November 1, 1879 -- Monterey, California

As Sean and Michael rode into town, Monterey appeared both sleepy and urban, the semblance of a growing American city, interspersed with the remnants of the once proud capital of Spanish and then Mexican Alta California, as well as an active, if small, Chinese district.

To Michael, it felt like several towns they had passed through in their travels, and yet like none of them, different in its own way.

Sean took note of the large number of saloons and gambling parlors lined up and down the main avenue. It immediately felt like his kind of town.

But first, they needed to turn the little girl over the town marshal, who turned out to be someone from their past.

"Bob!"

Marshal Roberto Fuentes looked up from his pile of paperwork and smiled. His hair was grayer, his midsection thicker, he no longer had his beard, and he had long since traded in his blue army uniform for a suit of civilian clothes. But his smile hadn't changed.

"Good Lord. I'd have thought you two would be dead by now."

"Not yet," Sean replied. "How did a reprobate like yourself ever become a city marshal?"

"I was elected. They like war heroes hereabouts."

"Even war heroes from the other side?"

"I wasn't fighting for the other side, when I left Monterey."

"Fair enough, Bob," Sean said.

"And it's still Roberto, Sean."

"Of course," Sean said in Spanish.

"So, what brings you two to the marshal's office? Confessing some crime you committed?"

"Heaven forbid," Sean said, crossing himself.

Michael brought the little girl forward. "We found this little one on the dunes south o' here. Her parents an' little brother were dead. Shot."

Roberto came around his desk to get a better look at the girl.

"Do ya know her?" Sean asked.

"No. But we've got a fair sized Chinese population in and about Monterey, especially out in the fishing village at Point Alones. She speak any English?"

"Hasn't opened her mouth, since we found her," Michael said.

"We buried the others," Sean told Roberto. "I don't know if we should've, but it seemed like the Christian thing to do."

43

"Well, the dunes are outside my jurisdiction. I'll notify the county sheriff, but I doubt he'll even look into it," Roberto said. "The Chinese don't rate very high on his list of priorities. In the meantime, you must both come home with me for lunch. I know my wife would like to meet you."

"It'd be our pleasure," Sean replied, with a big hungry grin.

"We also have a Chinese housekeeper, who might be able to get some information from the girl."

Katy Fuentes greeted her husband's old army *compañeros* warmly.

"Welcome! Roberto has told me so much about you."

"Really?" Sean replied, surprised.

"No. He never talks about the war."

Roberto shrugged. "We lost. What's to tell?"

Just then, their five year old granddaughter, Ana, appeared from a back room and gave her grandfather a great big hug around the legs.

"Grandpa Bob!" she exclaimed.

Sean and Michael both smiled.

"She can get away with calling me Bob."

"I'm sure she gets away with more than that," Sean said.

Roberto also introduced Sean and Michael to their attractive, middle-aged Chinese housekeeper, Ying, and asked her if she could get the little girl to tell them what happened on the dunes. It wasn't difficult.

As soon as Ying greeted her warmly in Cantonese, the little girl began talking rapidly and with wild emotion, like the words had been pent-up inside of her, since before she left China -- which, to a large extent, they had. Ying did her best to keep up with her in her translation.

"She says her name is Shushu, and she's from a village, where she lived with her family. Her father sold her to the Zhang family. They brought her here to marry Ping, when he got older. But she didn't like them. Madame Zhang punished her, and Ping bullied her."

"Do you know the Zhangs?" Roberto asked Ying.

Ying nodded. "They recently came to America to run a store in the Chinese village at Point Alones for their cousin, Master Lau, who also owns Lau's General Store in Chinatown."

"The Zhangs must have been the family on the beach," Roberto said.

"The beach?" Katy asked.

"We found the little girl next to a Chinese family on the beach," Sean told her. "They'd been killed."

"Dear God," Katy said, then crossed herself.

"Ask her what happened on the beach, yesterday," Roberto instructed.

"They were walking in the sand, and the Zhangs were far ahead of her, because they made her carry the food basket, and it was heavy. And she lost sight of them, because they were so far ahead. Then there was a lot of noise -- yelling and loud noise. By the time she caught up with the Zhangs -- they were dead."

"Did she see who shot the Zhangs?" Roberto asked.

Suddenly quiet and withdrawn, Shushu shook her head.

"What will ya do with her?" Michael asked.

"Well, the only people who appear to have any sort of claim on her in America would be the Laus," Roberto said. "If they want her."

"And if they don't?" Katy asked.

Roberto paused, then said, "Well, we'll take her to the Laus and see what they want to do."

No one knew exactly what to say next, until Sean noticed a fiddle resting on a shelf off to one side. "Which one of you plays the fiddle?" he asked.

"Ana's father did," Katy replied. "But he didn't stay with it."

"You used to play, Miguelito," Roberto remembered.

"Years ago," Michael said. "I haven't touched a bow since I can't remember when."

Katy picked up the instrument and offered it to Michael. "Would you like to try?"

"Yes, Señor Miguelito, please," Ana pleaded.

Michael looked at Ana, then at Katy, who nodded, encouragingly. He took the fiddle and held it carefully, then blew some dust off of it. Finally, he plucked the first string.

"It's a wee bit out o' tune."

Katy crossed over to a spinet piano that was covered with a large, colorful shawl.

"That's all right. So's my piano. But I think I can give you an approximation of the right note to tune it with."

Michael looked around the room at the expectant faces, then plucked the first string again.

Katy plunked on G below middle C, and Michael tightened the string to the pitch of the piano, then did the same for D, A, and E. Then he picked up the bow, tightened the hairs, and drew it across the strings.

He decided to attempt an Irish air, something simple, with not a lot of finger movement. It was a familiar tune for him, one he had played in both the American and Mexican army camps back in the day, one he had learned as a boy back in Donegal.

Shushu listened intently. The sound of the violin reminded her of her grandfather, when he played his *erhu*, a two-stringed Chinese fiddle, also played with a bow.

Michael's playing brought back Shushu's memories of a happier time in China, when her beloved grandfather, her *Yeh Yeh*, was still alive.

When Michael finished, everyone in the room applauded.

"Very good, Michaleen!" Sean called out. He was genuinely happy to see his friend playing the fiddle once again, and the delight it still gave him, even if he was a little rusty. "Encore!"

"Yes," Ana said. "Another, please."

"After lunch," Katy said.

Michael nodded, then looked down at Shushu, who was smiling back up at him. It was the first time he had seen her smile.

Ying noticed the smile as well. "Well, at least we've found one thing that makes Shushu smile -- music."

Michael smiled back at the little sprite.

"Begorah," he said just above a whisper.

Chapter Eight

November 1, 1879 -- Monterey

After the hearty lunch Katy and Ying had prepared, Michael played a couple more tunes on the fiddle, which elicited more smiles and even a giggle or two from both Shushu and Ana, while Sean and Roberto whispered back and forth remembrances of Michael's playing in the Mexican army camps, lifting the spirits of the soldiers after each hard fought and bloody defeat.

As the afternoon wore on, Roberto had the unpleasant duty to break up the happy reunion, as he needed to inform the Laus about the Zhangs and leave young Shushu with them. He asked Ying to come along for any necessary translation, so there would be no misunderstanding.

Sean and Michael asked to go along as well. They were curious to see what was going to happen to their temporary traveling companion.

The Laus ran a small, but well-stocked general store, that catered primarily to the residents of the Chinatown district along Franklin and Washington Streets, selling a combination of dry goods, imported Chinese products, fresh produce, homemade Chinese pastries -- which were a big seller -- and all the ingredients needed to fill a prescription from a Chinese herbal doctor, kept in a wall of drawers behind the main counter.

The Laus were a little older than the Zhangs and spoke enough pidgin English to understand what Marshal Fuentes told them. Master Lau kept a stoic composure, but Madame Lau broke down, especially when the marshal mentioned little Ping. Master Lau told Roberto, with Ying's help, how much they liked the Zhangs and how well they had run their new store in the fishing village at Point Alones for them.

Roberto, Michael, and Ying couldn't quite tell whether Lau was more upset about the deaths of the Zhangs, or that he no longer had anyone to run his new store for him, but they could see by the way the Laus looked at Shushu, they had little use for a little girl. She would just be another mouth to feed, but too young to help out much in the store. Still, she was family, more or less, so they reluctantly agreed it was their obligation to take her in.

While Roberto continued to tell the Laus what he knew about the death of the Zhangs, Sean became distracted by the noise in the store's back room, where Lau ran a gambling parlor, specializing in Chinese games of chance that were unfamiliar to Sean, but were eagerly played by Chinese men at a pair of tables.

"This game, here, is called *fan-tan*," Ying explained. "Two hands full of beans are laid on table and covered with a *tan koi*, the metal bowl over there. Players bet on how many beans will be left, then the *tan kun* removes the beans from

49

center of the table, always four at a time, until one, two, three, or four beans remain."

"The other game," Ying continued, "is called *pok-kop-pew*. It is like what you call a lottery. You pick characters on a ticket, then the announcer reads which characters are the winners."

Michael wondered how a Chinese woman would be so familiar with the rules to the games.

"My father like to play both games back in China," she told him.

"They seem to be more games of luck than skill," Sean observed.

"The Chinese believe it is better to be born lucky than clever," Ying explained.

"Luck's important," Sean conceded, "but skill separates men from their money."

Michael looked back at Shushu, who was standing all alone in the middle of the store, looking back at him.

"Take care, little sprite," he said, just above a whisper. "Take care."

Chapter Nine

1847 -- Mexico

In the five months that passed after the retreat from Monterrey, desertion grew to ominous numbers in the Mexican Army. The Mexican Republic had only been in existence for some twenty-five years, and most of the peasant-soldiers felt more of an allegiance to their family and their village than to their country.

Morale remained high amongst the Irish deserters in the San Patricios. They were proud of their success at Monterrey, even if it hadn't been enough to turn the tide of the battle. Now, with the heavy cannons President Santa Anna had issued them, they were certain the next battle would end in victory.

Sean, Michael, and Jamie learned more and more Spanish and felt more and more a kinship with their Mexican comrades. They danced with pretty señoritas at numerous fiestas and made love to a few of them as well.

But the American Army of Occupation was not going to wait for long. General Taylor could not afford to. He was hemorrhaging deserters himself, with immigrant-soldiers recently arrived from Ireland, Germany, Switzerland, Scotland, and Poland going over to the enemy, as well as several slaves who had fled from the southern states to Mexico and enlisted in the ever-increasingly multi-national San Patricios.

Taylor also received word that a second army, under the command of Winfield Scott, was preparing to land at Vera Cruz to steal his thunder.

President James K. Polk, a Democrat, worried that a victorious Zachary Taylor, a Whig, would prove to be a formidable political opponent in a future presidential election and sent Scott to establish a second front against the Mexicans. Scott even ordered Taylor to send many of his best troops east to bolster his ranks, including Sean, Michael, and Jamie's old company.

Santa Anna saw this as an opportunity and rushed his army back north to wipe out Taylor's diminished force, before turning his attention to Scott. And the San Patricios were in the vanguard. It was a brutal march, losing nearly a quarter of the soldiers to death, disease, or desertion, but the remaining troops were in high spirits, as they still outnumbered the Americans almost three to one.

The Mexicans found advance forces of Taylor's army, engineers, scouting out potential battle terrain in the Coahulla desert, concentrating on a valley halfway between the villages of Angostura and San Juan de la Buena Vista.

Lieutenant Riley sized up the location and decided the best spot for his cannons was on a ridge overlooking any potential American positions in the valley.

The problem was, the only path up to the ridge was a rugged escarpment, fine for a skilled horseman to climb, but much too steep for horses to pull the cannons. So, Jamie, Sean, Michael, and the rest of the San Patricios spent the better part of a day hauling the one-ton field pieces up onto the ridge, helped by two support companies of Mexican infantry.

The ridge, itself, was suited well enough for an artillery position, flat and deep enough, but it also contained a large number of snakes, rattlers, by the sounds of their tails making noise all about.

For the Irishmen, the only thing worse than being surrounded by rattlesnakes was not being able to see them -- only hear them.

"Damn creatures," Jamie cursed. "Where are they?"

Roberto smiled at Jamie, then took a good look around.

While the other soldiers watched, the bearded corporal followed the sound of the closest rattle, until he located a really big viper, clearly angry at this intrusion and commotion into its previously quiet space. It reared up and looked Roberto in the eye, hissing and scowling.

Roberto smiled back at the creature, while his best friend, Miguel, approached the snake from its right. Then, as the snake turned to look at Miguel, Roberto stepped on the creature's back, pulled a machete from his hip scabbard, and cut off its head in one quick motion.

"Sounds like there are more than enough snakes up here to make quite a feast," Roberto announced.

He sliced off the tail and tossed the body to Jamie, who caught it, ever so reluctantly. Then he held up the tail to show Sean and Michael.

"A present for my infant boy back home," Roberto said, then shook it so it rattled, like a child's toy.

Sean and Michael looked back at him in disbelief, which caused Roberto and the other Mexicans to laugh.

The Battle of Buena Vista -- known by the Mexicans as the Battle of Angostura -- was a pitched blood bath, in which the San Patricios dueled all day with the American cannon batteries, while infantry units from both sides were decimated in the crossfire.

Once again, Sean and Michael worked on the same crew, loading and firing one of the large cannons, becoming covered in soot and sweat, their arms and legs aching from the effort.

As they had at Monterrey, the Irishmen kept up their battlefield banter all through the battle, even as they lost over a third of their rank, killed or wounded by enemy shelling and rifle fire, including Michael, who took grape shot shrapnel that added even more scar tissue to the whip marks on his back.

Sean helped his friend away from the cannon.

"Does it hurt, Michaleen?"

"Of course it hurts," Michael answered back. "Though not as much as the whippin' I got from that bloody Baxter."

Sean stood up and shouted out at the Americans.

"Come on, Baxter! We're waitin' for ya! Give us a target to shoot at!"

Zachary Taylor became so exasperated by the effectiveness of the San Patricios, he ordered the 1st Dragoons to take the battery. Since the cannon muzzles could not be lowered sufficiently to direct their fire on the approaching dragoons, many of the Irishmen picked up muskets and joined the infantry supporting them to rain shot down on the mounted troops below.

By nightfall, both sides felt the Mexicans had won the battle, but Santa Anna added up the numbers and decided the pyrrhic victory had cost too many men to continue. Santa Anna needed every man he could assemble to face Winfield Scott's army, which was approaching Mexico City on the same route Cortez had taken three centuries before to conquer the Aztecs.

Santa Anna and Scott met at Cerro Gordo, where the San Patricios had to abandon their heaviest cannons after fierce hand-to-hand fighting.

Jamie Murphy was fearless, taking on enemy soldiers, one after another, shooting one with a musket he grabbed from a dead Mexican infantryman, then using the bayonet to stab and slash two more.

Sean wasn't quite as reckless as his friend, but was just as unwilling to be taken prisoner. He figured it would be better to die on the battlefield than languish in some prison cell, before being shot by a firing squad as a deserter.

The infantry company that supported them also fought bravely, but not having the sentence of death hanging over their heads like the deserters, they began to lose their nerve and fall back, first one by one, then in groups. Corporal Fuentes was one of the last to leave, insisting Sean and Jamie do the same.

With only four cannons left, the San Patricios were reorganized as an infantry battalion, the Foreign Legion of San Patricios, under the command of Colonel Francisco Moreno and Brevet Major John Riley, and were issued Brown Bess muskets to fight with.

The San Patricios fell back to establish a defensive position in front of the former Franciscan monastery of Santa Maria de Los Angeles, just five miles outside of Mexico City, with the *Batallón de Independencia* on their right and the *Batallón de Bravo* on their left, while the rest of the Mexican Army fought and lost another battle at Padierna, before retreating through the rainy night to join their Irish comrades at this new position at Churubusco, an Aztec word that meant the "place of the war god," an appropriate location for a last stand.

Michael returned to duty from his stay in a traveling field hospital, but since his wounds had not entirely healed, Major Riley assigned him and Sean to see to it the gunpowder for the cannons and muskets stayed dry from the rain in the supply wagon under the oil-treated canvas tarpaulins.

Major Riley walked slowly, back and forth, behind the four cannons, chatting with the men, trying to keep their spirits up and their minds off the upcoming battle.

At one point, halfway between midnight and dawn, Riley walked over to Sean.

"You haven't recited that poem of yours lately, Mulcahy," Riley said, "have ya."

"No, sir," Sean said.

Riley then looked at Michael, but didn't say anything. He didn't have to.

Michael opened the wooden case and took out his fiddle and bow, then tucked the instrument under his chin.

Sean began to recite the poem as he had several times before, emphasizing the ironic dark humor intended in the piece.

"As the north wind blows, so the story goes,
The Irish never planned to leave their home.
Then England set 'em straight,
Told 'em . . ."

"Travelin' was great!'" the Irishmen shouted in unison.

"An' set the Gaels a-startin' for to roam." said Sean.

By the time he started the second verse, Michael had already begun to draw his horse hair bow across the strings, adding a plaintive accompaniment.

"The story then goes on, so many Gaels had gone,
For English rule encouraged Irish flight.
The Ulster Earls to Spain, Wild Geese to Aquitaine,
Where e're the Irish went, they found a fight."

Each verse became ever more poignant and hit closer to home with the remaining San Patricios, whose thoughts went back to their families back in Ireland and their comrades who fell in previous battles.

"So the chronicles unfold, the sordid tale is told,
How 'merica ne'er succumbed to Gaelic charms.
For us they had no use, an' heaped on us abuse.
While Mexico welcomed us with open arms."

At the end of his recital, Sean paused for a moment, then added a new verse for his assembled comrades:

"Our tale comes to a close, the San Patricios,
The legendary Wild Geese who then chose,
To make this final stand, fallen brothers close at hand.
We, last of all the San Patricios!

A spontaneous cheer went up from the remaining members of the battalion, with fists raised defiantly. Major Riley nodded his silent approval.

By morning, the rain had stopped, and Sean and Michael started to issue out the powder and shot to the crews of the four cannons. By noon, a cloud of dust could be seen up the road leading to the monastery.

As the enemy came into view, the San Patricios held their fire, while Major Riley raised their green flag. They continued to hold their fire, as the enemy got to what looked like they were no more than a hundred yards away.

When they got to within sixty yards, Riley gave the command. The four cannons and the row of muskets opened fire, decimating the columns of soldiers, turning their light blue tunics red with blood.

For three hours, the Irish deserters and their Mexican *compañero de armes* shredded the enemy. The Irish took particular delight in targeting American junior officers, who had inflicted the tortuous punishment that drove them to desert in the first place. A fair number of lieutenants and captains died that afternoon before the monastery.

Jamie caught sight of Sergeant Baxter, who had performed the whipping that killed Patrick Kelly. The Irishman aimed one of the cannons right at him and fired a round of grape shot, which tore the sergeant to shreds, along with the nativist lieutenant, who had ordered the punishment, for good measure.

By three o'clock, three of Irish cannons were out of commission, but Major Riley urged the last cannon crew to keep up their fire. Then, as Jamie reached for one of the last canisters of grape from the supply wagon, a spark from who knows where ignited the last of the gunpowder and turned the wagon into a fireball, incinerating Michael's fiddle, and killing everyone close to the explosion, including Jamie Murphy.

The San Patricios were being cut to pieces. All around them, Sean and Michael's comrades were dead or seriously wounded.

One of the exhausted soldiers from the *Batallón de Bravo* tried to raise a white flag, but was immediately stopped by Sean.

"You can leave the field, boyo," Sean told him, "but we can't surrender!"

After the last cannon had been destroyed, Sean picked up a musket. Michael spied a lever-action Colt revolver on the ground and grabbed it. He aimed it at an approaching soldier and fired, hitting him square in the chest.

"You're certainly better with a hand gun than a musket," Sean called out, before he impaled another incoming soldier with his bayonet.

"I can shoot the bloody thing with my left hand," Michael yelled back, then fired off another round.

Having done all they could, Major Riley ordered the few remaining San Patricios to pull back behind the monastery walls, before he fell, severely wounded.

As Michael rushed to prevent the San Patricios colors from being captured by the enemy, he didn't notice Sean being hit with a bullet in his left hip.

"Damn it to bloody hell!"

Michael looked back and saw Sean on the ground, writhing in pain. His first instinct was to go back after him, but the American soldiers had overrun the field. There was nothing he could do.

Michael fired the hand gun one last time, then he and Roberto retreated into the monastery without their friend.

Chapter Ten

November 1, 1879 -- Monterey, California

After they left Shushu with the Laus, and Ying returned to the Fuentes home, Roberto escorted Sean and Michael toward the French Hotel.

"You'll like the French. It's clean and quiet. Owned by Manuela Giradins, a sweet little old lady, and run by her daughter, Marie, and son-in-law, John Heintz, who also happens to be a doctor -- in case you have another bad reaction to a chili pepper, Sean."

As they came on the town square, they found a short, angry Irishman standing on a small, elevated platform, spouting diatribes about how evil the Chinese were, and how they should be kicked out of California.

"Who's that?" Sean asked.

"Denis Kearney," Roberto replied. "Head of the Workingman's Party, an anti-Chinese labor organization.

He's been trying to organize a branch here in Monterey for over a year now, without much success."

In fact, Kearney had only drawn a small crowd, and many of those didn't even bother to hear him finish, including a pleasant-looking fellow in a tailored suit and a big, burly man with a badge on his jacket.

"Sean, Michael," Roberto said, "this is State Senator Walter Maguire and Fred Lang, sheriff of Monterey County."

Walter smiled, as he shook hands with the two strangers. "Welcome to Monterey."

"Like the speech?" Lang asked.

"Fred, these are guests in our community," Walter said. "We should make them feel welcome, not overwhelm them with politics."

Fred scowled at the senator.

"What's wrong with the Chinese?" Michael asked.

"They take jobs away from white folks," Fred told him.

"I thought they were a large part of the crew that built the railroad from California to Utah," Michael said.

"They did their job," Lang said. "Now they can go home."

"And you, Senator?" Sean asked.

"Me? Well, I believe in free speech. But I also believe we're all God's children."

"That's the thing about politicians," Fred said. "You can know a guy for thirty years, then he becomes a politician, and he gets holier than thou."

"Easy enough for you, Fred. You never go to church."

"Don't mind them," came a female voice from behind them.

Walter and Fred turned aside to reveal an attractive, older woman in a well-tooled, tailored riding jacket and matching skirt, smiling at them.

"He may be a competent state senator, and he may be an adequate county sheriff, but they argue all the time. Some friends do that."

"Gentlemen," Walter said. "I'd like to introduce you to my sister, Olivia Connolly."

"Another one of our civic leaders," Roberto added.

"Only one?" Olivia said, feigning indignation.

"Our most important civic leader," Roberto said, correcting himself, with a sly smile.

"He only says that, because my bank holds the mortgage on his ranch outside of town," she said.

"My retirement ranch," Roberto explained. "When my term as marshal is over next year."

"So, you're definitely not going to run for reelection?" Walter asked.

Roberto nodded, without any sign of doubt or regret.

Michael looked back at Kearney, who seemed to be building to his conclusion.

"And whatever happens, the Chinese must go!"

The small crowd cheered and applauded his speech, while Kearney stepped down and shook a few hands.

"Wasn't that long ago people said that kinda thing about the Irish," Michael said.

"I remember all too well," Olivia said. "Some of it still exists back east."

"Is that why you came west?" Sean asked, with a smile.

Olivia took a moment to size up the handsome, if scruffy, newcomer, then returned the smile.

"That's a story to tell over a drink."

Everyone agreed, but Roberto, who waved off.

"I've heard your story, and I should get back to my pile of paperwork."

"I'm buying," Olivia said.

"Well, the pile isn't that high."

The group retired to a saloon just off the square, where Olivia bought a round of beers.

"My husband and I came west in Forty-Nine," she began.

"Prospectin'?" Sean asked.

"Heavens, no," she said. "We ran a saloon and gambling tent in the mining camps. That's where the real money was. We came west in a covered wagon, with decks of playing cards, boxes of poker chips, and cases of whiskey, then moved from mining camp to mining camp, following the miners through the gold country. We made a fortune. Thanks, in part, to Walter, here."

Olivia touched Walter's hand, affectionately.

"I just supplied them with a little money to expand their operation," Walter said. "George and Olivia did all the work. It worked out well for all of us."

Walter and Olivia both smiled. Michael noticed Fred didn't join them. He held onto a serious expression, with, perhaps, a trace of resentment or jealousy.

Sean looked at Walter. "You come out with your sister?"

"No. Fred and I came to California with the Seventh New York Volunteers during the Mexican War, while Roberto, here, was down in Mexico."

Fred laughed.

"He left Monterey a Mexican soldier to fight the American Army -- and returned to Monterey an American citizen! How's that for irony?"

Sean and Michael looked at their friend, who glanced back at them, with a wry smile, before he took another sip of beer.

Olivia, meanwhile, was annoyed with the way Fred had poked fun at the city marshal.

"Anyway -- after my husband died, I settled here in Monterey and got into more respectable enterprises -- banking and real estate. It wasn't as exciting as dealing faro, but I had a son to look after, and he needed a place to go to school."

Roberto's attention had been drawn to an argument developing at a table across the room. Two men, who had obviously had too much to drink, became louder and louder, arguing over some pointless triviality.

Drunken arguments were common enough in saloons, and this one seemed no different from a hundred others.

Then they had to go for their guns.

The two men may have worn guns, but they weren't gunmen. They fired wildly, completely missing one another, even though they were only a few feet apart. They seemed much more afraid of getting shot than shooting accurately, taking cover behind the nearest table or chair.

They continued to fire back and forth, endangering the lives of everyone else in the saloon. At least two stray shots had already hit bystanders.

Roberto got to his feet and pulled his revolver.

"Stop it!" He called out. "Right now!"

Sean glanced over at Sheriff Lang, who remained seated.

"City business," Lang said, flatly.

Michael quietly lifted the small leather loop off the hammer of his revolver, then removed his spectacles to wipe off any smudges with his pocket handkerchief -- just in case.

Roberto fired off a round, a marksman caliber shot, which hit one of the miscreants in the shoulder. The other man wheeled around and pointed his gun in Roberto's general direction.

"Drop it now!" the marshal told him.

The second man pulled back the hammer on his pistol, ignoring Roberto's command, leaving the marshal no choice, but to shoot him square in the chest.

The first man held his bloody shoulder with his left hand, while slowly raising his pistol with his right, pointing it in Roberto's general direction. Roberto didn't hesitate. He fired again, killing him.

"This is a part of the job I won't miss," Roberto said, as he returned his revolver to his holster.

Just then, a third fellow, most likely a friend of one of the two would-be gunfighters, got to his feet.

"Bastard!" he yelled, as he went for his pistol.

He'd barely cleared his holster, when Michael shot him through the heart. He was dead before he hit the floor.

"Not a bad shot for a man who wears spectacles," Roberto noted.

Michael let a smile crease his lips, then twirled the revolver on his index finger, before sliding it back into his holster and reattaching the small leather loop over the hammer.

The marshal walked across the saloon to get a better look at the carnage, while Sheriff Lang finished off his beer.

Chapter Eleven

1846 -- New York

Walter Maguire's father was the first to hear about the new unit being formed: the 7th Regiment of New York Volunteers, to be made up of respectable, young, unmarried men from various backgrounds and training, under the command of Colonel Jonathan D. Stevenson, late of the New York State Assembly. They were being sent to help defeat the Mexicans in California.

Walter's mother was the one who encouraged him to sign up, even though she knew she'd probably never see him again. After serving their time, the volunteers understood they would be mustered out in California to increase the American population in the region and help more quickly transform California into an American territory and future state of the Union.

His mother had emigrated to America as a young woman, leaving her family behind in County Fermanagh, and found work as a scrub woman, until she met and fell in love with a third generation Irish-American cobbler, whose grandfather had fought with Benedict Arnold at Saratoga.

The 7th Regiment left New York harbor on September 27, 1846, aboard four ships and traveled south, around Cape Horn, on their way to California.

During the long voyage, Walter became friends with a tall, muscular fellow, who won every boxing match he fought on the ship and made Walter a lot of money betting on him, which he shared with the boxer.

The youngest of four sons of a well-to-do family, Frederick Lang hated working at the family's import-export business and hated even more working under his much older brother, whom their father had made managing director. Fred wanted to make his own way in the world, make his fortune beholding to no one -- and away from his detested tyrant of an older brother.

Fred and Walter talked about the opportunities that might be found in California. The only thing they knew for certain was that shoemaking and the import-export business were out of the question.

"We aren't traveling all the way to California to go back to what we could have done back in New York," Fred said on more than one occasion.

The argument appealed to Walter, who had already come to the same conclusion before they left New York.

The ships arrived in San Francisco in March, 1847, two months after Lieutenant Colonel John C. Frémont and Acting Governor Andrés Pico had signed a truce, ending hostilities in California. Consequently, the soldiers of the 7th were assigned garrison duty in Monterey, Santa Barbara, Los Angeles, and San Diego, and the unit was renamed the 1st Regiment of New York Volunteers.

Walter and Fred were stationed at the Monterey Presidio, the former royal Spanish fort that was suppose to protect the capital of Alta California from invaders.

Fred continued to engage in boxing matches, for sport and profit, but he soon discovered some of the rough and rugged mountain men that had captured California with Frémont were a lot tougher than the working class fellows that made up the New York Volunteers. Fred didn't entirely give up accepting boxing challenges, but Walter gave up betting on him.

Meanwhile, while they served their tour of garrison duty, they kept their eyes and ears open for any big financial opportunities.

The first one came in January, 1848, when gold was discovered along the South Fork American River -- at Sutter's Mill.

Fred and Walter were among the first to stake a claim and pan for pretty much anything shiny they could find buried in the mud and silt. They became partners, protecting each other's back, and splitting whatever gold they found right down the middle.

It was hard work, and the two young men had quite a lot to learn about prospecting, such as discovering the difference between pyrite and the real thing, and how to build bigger and better sluice boxes that separated out the gold more efficiently. But the two New York city boys took to the outdoor life, even sleeping out under the stars during the summer and discussing how they would spend their fortunes.

"I wanna buy a big piece of property," Fred said, "with a big yard, all fenced off, and a big house, three stories high."

"I want to be important," Walter said. "A senator or governor. Someone people look up to."

"Why?"

"I want to be remembered."

"Why?' Fred repeated.

Walter smiled. "Why not?"

"Tell you what, you be important; I'll be powerful. You can be looked up to; I'll be feared."

They shook on that proposal.

As the weather cooled, the two partners built a cabin, that leaked like a sieve during the first wind-swept thunderstorm that came along. They thought they had patched all the holes, but it continued to leak, when the next storm hit. Fortunately, they found a carpenter working a claim down river, who patched the cabin's ceiling well enough to withstand the elements.

They formed friendships with most of the prospectors in their vicinity, including immigrants from Mexico and even from China, who had heard of the discovery and traveled across the Pacific to reach the *Gum San*, the "Gold Mountain".

Walter and Fred learned how to make tortillas and a dozen ways to cook fish and wild fowl from the wives of their immigrant neighbors, who had accompanied their husbands and helped pan for gold. Eventually, they hired the teenage daughter of a Mexican prospector to cook for them.

These friendships were essential, beyond the camaraderie. The area was lawless, beyond the property claimed by the rancheros in the Mexican land grants, and caught in the period between the end of Mexican law and the establishment of American courts, with a constant threat of claim jumpers, trying to steal their stake, and highwaymen, who just wanted to steal their gold. Justice was meted out by those who fired first and most effectively, and the most reliable allies the two men could have were the ones who had their own claims to protect, no matter what their nationalities might be.

Fred found he had a talent for carnage. He never drew a weapon or pointed a musket, except to kill. He was fearless in the face of overwhelming odds, firing away without regard for how much ammunition he had left, protecting his Mexican and Chinese friends and, especially, his partner. Walter never had to worry about his limited ability with a firearm.

"That's my job, ole buddy," Fred said on more than one occasion, after he shot and killed a would-be claim jumper.

As 1849 progressed, thousands more came to the California gold fields, looking for their own fortunes, although not all of them sought it panning for gold. Merchants set up shops, selling goods to the prospectors at inflated prices and considerable profits.

Fred spent his new-found wealth almost as quickly as he collected it on gambling and liquor and prostitutes, while Walter quickly realized that, at the end of the day, the merchants were making more money than the prospectors and didn't work nearly as hard -- or got shot at by thieves or claim jumpers.

That appealed to Walter.

Chapter Twelve

November 1, 1879 -- Monterey, California

After the shoot-out in the saloon, Sean took it upon himself to escort Olivia down the street to her bank. Like Sean, she didn't like the sight of gunplay, but had spent enough time running saloons to witness more than her fair share. And she liked the attention of the good-looking stranger, whose first instinct wasn't to draw his own revolver.

As they walked along, they could see the construction of a new building, a full three stories above anything else in Monterey.

"It's going to be the Hotel Del Monte," Olivia told him, "being built by Charles Crocker, president of the Southern Pacific Railroad. First, he built rail lines to Monterey from Sacramento, Salinas, and San Francisco . . ."

"Now he's building an elegant hotel where the train passengers can stay," Sean added. "Brilliant."

"The future of Monterey is tourism, Mr. Mulcahy."

"Well, if Mr. Crocker is spending all that money on a fancy hotel, he must know something."

"Do you know anything about the tourist business, Mr. Mulcahy?" Olivia asked.

"Well, I know a great deal about travel," he said. "For instance, one of the best reasons to stay somewhere, instead of just passin' through, is a great place to eat. What would ya say is the best restaurant in Monterey?"

"My personal favorite would be Carmen's. It has the best Mexican food this side of Los Angeles."

"In that case, would ya do me the honor of havin' dinner with me tonight at Carmen's, Mrs. Connolly?"

Olivia paused, then smiled. "Yes, Mr. Mulcahy. I think I will. You may pick me up at the bank at seven o'clock."

"Seven o'clock? Ya work late."

"I'm president of the bank."

Sean smiled, kissed the back of her hand, then watched, as Olivia passed through the bank's front entrance, pausing long enough to glance back at him.

Sean was waiting at the bank's entrance precisely at seven in a freshly brushed suit and took Olivia by the arm, escorting her down the street to Carmen's Cantina, a quiet, unassuming restaurant, family owned, using Grandma Carmen's well-crafted recipes for every dish served.

Sean spent the evening spinning yarn after yarn of his adventures, leaving out some of his more illicit activities, which he felt were inappropriate for a first date. She was, after all, a lady and an upstanding member of the community.

Olivia Maguire Connolly did not get many dinner invitations, and most of those were business-related. As one of the richest and most powerful women in the county, she intimidated most of the men she met, whether she meant to or not -- and more often than not she had meant to.

In an age when women were second-class citizens, not even allowed to vote, she felt she needed an edge to succeed in her diverse business enterprises.

But, like most other women, she enjoyed the attention of a handsome man with manners and a degree of wit and intelligence, which Sean Mulcahy had in abundance.

In many ways, Sean reminded her of her late husband, who had also been a smooth-talking, wheeler-dealing adventurer. Like her husband, he was an expert of the well-timed compliment. She could easily see through his blarney, but she enjoyed it, nonetheless.

After dinner, Sean walked Olivia to the livery stable across the street from the bank, where she kept her horse and buggy, which she drove to her ranch, southeast of town, near the base of the Santa Lucia Highlands.

Olivia was surprised to find her younger brother, Liam, in the front parlor, asleep in one of her over-stuffed chairs.

"What are you doing here?" she asked. "You're suppose to be in Salinas."

Liam got up poured himself a whiskey. "I finished in Salinas."

"You got all the deed transfers recorded with the county?"Olivia asked.

"Yep! You can throw those Chinks out of their crappy fishing village any time ya want."

"I will not have talk like that in my house," she said, angrily. "I'm not anti-Chinese; I'm not anti-anybody. They're just in the way of progress. When Crocker opens his hotel, the guests are going to want to have something to do, when they visit Monterey, like carriage rides along our spectacular coastline. Then perhaps more hotels, more restaurants and shops, built on our land, where they can spend their money.

The Chinese can move their village further down the coast."

"It's a good thing California won't let the Chinese own land," Liam said. "Then again, people have been taking other people's property since the dawn of time. Hell, our people would have never left Ireland, if the English hadn't taken their land."

Olivia poured herself a brandy from the decanter on the side table.

"Is my son home?"

"No. He's out with his friends, drinking and whoring, no doubt."

Olivia looked disapprovingly at her brother.

"Well, it *IS* Saturday night," he volunteered.

"He just spent three days in San Luis Obispo with his friends, drinking and whoring."

Liam smiled. "Yeah, that's the town for it. Wide open."

"I'm surprised he had any money left after his trip. Did he ask for any?"

"No. Had money of his own, which he proudly proclaimed, before he left."

"Where did he get it?"

"Didn't say exactly, but I saw Sheriff Lang on the way back from Salinas, and he told me that Marshal Fuentes told him about some Chinese family that was killed on the dunes south of town yesterday. Wouldn't be surprised if George an' those two friends of his did it, on their way back from San Luis Obispo."

"Oh no. Are you sure?"

"Well, he didn't come right out an' admit to it, but you know how your son likes to brag about any stupid, so-called accomplishment."

Olivia swallowed her brandy, then sat in her other over-stuffed easy chair.

"Oh, an' he told me not to tell you. Like I keep secrets from my big sister."

"I raised an idiot, Liam. A shallow, short-sighted, addle-minded idiot. If it weren't too late for me to have more children, I'd smother him with a pillow in his own bed, while he was passed out drunk -- for his own good."

Olivia rose and crossed back to the brandy decanter to pour herself another drink. "This is about the future of Monterey. Are we going to become the tourist haven we want it to be -- or are we going to remain a backwater hamlet, where people can't even take a walk along our shoreline, without being accosted or killed?"

"They were only Chinese, Sis. The sheriff doesn't even care."

"That's not the point, Liam. A grisly attack like that reflects badly on the community -- and could jeopardize all of our investments!"

Chapter Thirteen

1847 -- Mexico

Sean Mulcahy was tried for desertion in a shabby, dilapidated warehouse in the town of Tacubaya and sentenced to be hung, along with the other San Patricios that had been captured at Churubusco. They would not even be afforded the usual military punishment of a firing squad. They weren't considered worthy enough.

The verdicts were then submitted to General Winfield Scott, who had to sign off on all military executions under his command.

He had no problem executing men who had deserted after war had been declared, but being a trained lawyer, he knew that the American Articles of War did not permit the execution of deserters in time of peace, and a number of the San Patricios, including Sean, had deserted before war had been declared.

Consequently, Scott changed the punishment of any man who had deserted before May 13, 1846 to a flogging of fifty lashes with a rawhide whip, then branded with a letter 'D' on their right cheek.

The sentence was carried out on a hill outside the village of Mixcoac, under the command of a particularly vicious disciplinarian, Colonel William Harney.

Harney was ordered to hang thirty of the condemned men on the hill top, that overlooked the American assault of Chapultepec Castle, just outside Mexico City, which would prove to be the last battle of the war. The condemned men were forced to stand on mule carts, with their arms tied behind their backs and nooses around their necks, facing Chapultepec in the distance, until the Americans successfully took the castle.

Meanwhile, as the battle raged, punishment was meted out on nine early deserters, including Sean Mulcahy, by Mexican muleteers, who were extremely skilled with a braided bullwhip.

Sean cried out as the twisted rawhide cut into his back. He fought hard to repeatedly catch his breath, as each stroke seemed to knock the wind right out of him. He cursed and screamed and struggled against the ropes tied to his wrists, to no avail. The flogging continued, stroke after blistering stroke.

Then came the branding. An iron had been heating up in a campfire nearby, with a two inch letter 'D', now a bright, red glow.

The prisoners had had their faces shaved particularly close that morning. Colonel Harney wanted the iron to make its mark on a clean surface.

Weak from the whipping, Sean's face was pressed against a tree, with his left cheek scraping against the bark, while the branding iron was pressed firmly against his right cheek.

The intense, indescribable pain of the red hot iron was nothing like Sean could ever have imagined. He screamed in agony and nearly passed out.

After standing on the mule wagons for over three hours, with the nooses around their necks and taunting Colonel Harney with a gallows' bravado, the thirty condemned men could finally make out, through the smoke of battle, the Mexican flag being lowered from the uppermost point on the castle and the Stars and Stripes replacing it on the flag pole.

Harney gave the order, the muleteers led their carts away, and the thirty San Patricios were hung before their comrades' eyes.

The nine survivors were returned to the Acordada Prison, along with seven bloodied and branded survivors of a second trial held in San Angel. Later, they were all moved to cells in the Chapultepec Castle.

Finally, after General Scott returned to the United States to a hero's welcome, General William Butler, his successor as commander-in-chief of the occupation forces, issued an order for the release of the twelve San Patricios still alive, nine months after they had been captured at Churubusco.

Michael found his friend in a military hospital in Mexico City.

He and the few San Patricios who had escaped capture at Churubusco had been camped out in the city of Querétaro, northwest of Mexico City. They were still, technically, in the Mexican Army, although the San Patricios as a unit had been disbanded, and the federal government was in such a state of disarray, the soldiers hadn't gotten paid in months.

Sean was an emaciated shell of his former self. What with the poor food the prisoners were fed, the minimal medical care he received for the bullet wound in his left hip, the hard, stone floors they were forced to sleep upon, and the hard labor they were ordered to perform almost every day, he had lost a good deal of weight.

But he had regained his spirit. He had survived the ordeal, lived to see another day, and the future seemed ripe with possibilities.

"Ah, Michaleen," Sean waxed poetically. "These past nine months, I swear, it felt like death was just sittin' there in the shadows, waitin' to take me away, even after they decided to whip an' brand me, instead of hang me, like they did so many of our comrades -- thank the Lord we deserted before war was declared -- an' they stuck us in that hellish prison to rot -- an' four did just that, God have mercy on their souls. But I had a conversation with God every night, as I laid down on that poor excuse of a straw mat they called a bed, with my poor hip racked with pain, thankin' Him for another day, an' dreamin' o' what I'd do, when I got out o' there."

Sean rattled off a list of contradictory things he wanted to do next. He wanted to travel. He wanted to be a man of property. He wanted to be rich. He wanted to teach Michael how to read.

"English or Spanish?" Michael asked.

"Let's start with English," Sean replied. "Then we can both learn to read Spanish."

But, most of all, Sean wanted to make love to beautiful women all over Mexico. "Women love war heroes, Michaleen," he said with a smile.

Michael could not help but stare at the 'D' branded onto his friend's right cheek. Sean had begun to grow a beard, hoping to cover it, but, of course, the skin directly under the brand was dead tissue that would never again allow hair to grow from it. Still, Sean reasoned, if the beard was bushy enough, he might be able to comb it over the scar.

Michael also grew a beard, partially because he had never grown one before, and, partially, because he didn't like showing off his unbranded cheek in front of his friend.

Sean repeatedly told Michael it wasn't his fault he had been captured.

"Why was I wounded at Churubusco, and you were at Angostura? Why weren't we both blown to bits along with Jamie, when the supply wagon exploded? We were unloadin' it with him. We just happened to be far enough away, handin' out ammunition to our comrades, when it went up. It's nobody's fault, Michaleen. Just the fortunes an' misfortunes of war."

Michael nodded -- but he still felt guilty about having left his friend behind.

While Sean took his time recovering -- and flirting with the pretty nurses who attended to him -- Michael found an old English primer in a dry goods store and, with his friend's help, taught himself how to read.

Michael had never had any schooling. Back in Donegal, a person learned how to toss nets, mend nets, and work an oar in a currach. That was enough to put food on the table -- until the potato famine destroyed the country.

But he had always wanted to learn to read, and it opened a whole new world for him. Michael took to reading pretty much anything he could find -- and read them almost every night.

Chapter Fourteen

November 1, 1879 -- Monterey

After the shoot-out in the saloon, Roberto instructed his deputy to collect the bodies of the three men and leave them at the office of Dr. Heintz, who served as the city coroner. He also briefed Lang about the killings of the Zhangs, before the sheriff returned to the county seat of Salinas.

Roberto then returned to his office with Michael, so he could take his friend's statement for the record. It was a formality, but Michael did shoot the third man.

Afterwards, the marshal began to get back to that pile of paperwork he told Olivia he needed to attend to, when he got a message the mayor wanted a quick word with him before he went home for dinner. Roberto knew the mayor's idea of a quick word usually meant a three-hour discussion. So he left the paperwork with his deputy, Ernesto, and went to see the mayor in his office on the second floor of the city hall.

The mayor got right to the point. "So, you've definitely decided not to run for re-election next year?"

"It's time. I'm almost sixty. Time to retire."

"Then who do we run as your replacement?"

"My deputy, Ernesto. He's a good man."

"He hasn't got your personality or your war record."

"Most of the citizens of Monterey weren't even born, when I fought in Mexico."

"You were highly decorated. And this is still essentially a Mexican pueblo."

The mayor stepped out on his balcony and looked out over the town, while he began to speak in Spanish.

"Spanish is spoken in more parts of town than English. I need someone with me on the ticket that people look up to."

"I thought that was your job," Roberto answered him back in Spanish.

"The Yanquis want to make Monterey into some quaint tourist attraction," the mayor continued in Spanish, "and all of us will become freaks for the rich Anglos from San Francisco or from back east to gawk at in our funny sombreros and serapes."

"Neither of us wear sombreros or serapes," Roberto pointed out.

"If the Anglos have their way, we may have to start."

Roberto leaned onto the balcony's railing, then looked out over his beloved hometown.

"Monterey has always adjusted to change and still been able to maintain its unique personality."

The mayor remained unconvinced.

"Look at us," Roberto said. "We were both born Spanish, when Monterey was part of New Spain, the capital of Alta California. Then, when Mexico broke away from Spain, we became Mexican citizens -- and nothing much changed.

82

Then, when I went away to fight the Americans in the south, I returned home to discover we had become American citizens. But we're still the same people. Older, but the same. And this is still the same Monterey."

The mayor sighed. "For now."

Later that night, another political meeting was held in a Salinas alley with six aging white men.

"What are we going to do about Denis Kearney?" Rancher Humphreys demanded to know.

"What's wrong with Kearney?" Sheriff Lang asked.

"His anti-Chinese party is stirring up resentment against the Chinese."

"What's wrong with that?"

"I need Chinese laborers to work my fields," Rancher Baker said. "I can't get any whites to work them -- or Mexicans, for that matter."

"Don't worry about Kearney," Senator Maguire said. "He serves a useful purpose. He keeps the working class preoccupied. Easterners got it into their heads they're special. I blame it on Manifest Destiny. The poor came west expecting wealth would be handed to them on a golden platter. And when it wasn't, they couldn't chalk it up to their own naïveté. It had to be somebody else's fault. And those of us who got here first, directed their attention at the rancheros, who were hogging all the land for themselves. Then it was the Mexicans who refused to go back to Mexico after California became a state. So what if they were born here? They were an easy scapegoat, when the economy went south. We couldn't have the poor blame the rich and powerful. Better to blame the greasers. And the Chinese. They don't look like us. They don't talk like us. They don't even dress like us. No matter they only do jobs no self-respecting white or Mexican would take.

They still take jobs. It makes no sense, but people believe it."

Senator Maguire looked over at the young Chinese man standing on a tall stool, his hands tied behind his back, a gag in his mouth, his eyes filled with terror, and a noose wrapped around his neck.

"We keep the Chinamen in line by preventing their women and children from emigrating, to give them a reason to go back to China. And those who have the presumption to try and sleep with a white woman while they're here . . ."

Maguire kicked the stool out from under the young Chinese man, then watched, as the noose tightened around his neck.

"That's my job, Walter," Fred said.

Sheriff Lang pulled his gun and shot the hapless young man in the chest.

"Shot trying to escape."

Walter was annoyed that his old friend had ruined his fun, but let it pass.

"Let the poor whites have their scapegoats," Walter continued, "so long as it's not us. Meanwhile, we will continue to allow just enough Chinese to remain in California to suit our needs."

Walter turned toward the back entrance of the one Chinese brothel in Salinas. "Like the five lovely young ladies who occupy this house of ill repute. Now, if you'll excuse me, I intend to partake of one of their celestial delights."

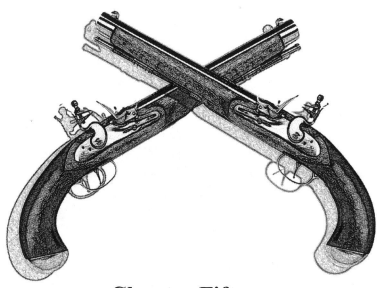

Chapter Fifteen

1850s -- California

On September 9, 1850, California became the thirty-first state of the Union. By then, the Yanquis from the east had taken control of the legislature, the governor's office, and, especially, the newly assembled courts, which regularly dismissed the legality of the old Mexican land grants for the vast ranchos.

Having run their claim dry of gold, Walter and Fred joined one of the roving, vigilante posses being financed by the wealthy Yanquis to string up the young Californios who were fighting back on the massive land and power grab by the Anglo newcomers.

Fred took to the life of the roving posse avenger. It paid well, and it suited his violent nature.

"The rich and powerful never do their own dirty work, ole buddy," he told Walter, "but they pay well enough for others to do it."

"We all have our strengths," Walter said. "And weaknesses."

Walter didn't really have the stomach for vigilantism, but saw it a means to an end. He knew that the breakup of the extensive ranchos would be an opportunity for him to invest some of his gold in land. And Walter was always on the lookout for something to invest in and increase his wealth.

As they passed through one of the many mining camps in the Sierra Nevada mountains, Walter was surprised and delighted to find his little sister, Olivia, and her husband, George, operating a modest saloon and gambling table under a large canvas tent next to a covered wagon.

To Walter, this was exactly what he was looking for. With a little capital, George and Olivia were able to construct a proper saloon building, stock it with kegs of beer from San Francisco, and add a second faro table to separate miners from even more of their gold. They even installed one of those long mirrors behind the bar, so drinkers could see who was coming up behind them -- and that always got shot up or shattered in the inevitable saloon brawl.

Walter tried to talk Fred into investing as well, but it sounded too much like getting involved in a family business, which was why he left New York in the first place.

Instead, he continued to ride with the roving posse.

The traveling saloon and gambling business proved to be quite profitable for George and Olivia -- and for Walter, who then used his profits to buy shares in the Central Pacific Railroad for himself and his sister. That was even more profitable. Then he married the daughter of a rich landowner, and her dowry made him considerably richer.

Fred also bought a few shares in the Central Pacific Railroad, though not nearly as many as Walter.

Fred also married the sister of a rich landowner, with a respectable dowry, but no real chance of inheriting her brother's land.

When her husband died of a fever, Olivia took her young son, George, Jr., and settled in the town of Monterey, where she used her considerable assets from the traveling saloon and railroad investments to open a small bank, specializing mainly in real estate loans, something in which she became quite adroit.

Fred settled in the more Anglicized town of Salinas, which eventually became the county seat of Monterey, and he successfully ran for County Sheriff, promising law and order, especially order.

He finally did build his three-story house with a fence surrounding his property, but it wasn't nearly as grand as he had envisioned it -- and he could only make it happen by taking out a large mortgage, which was held by the bank owned by Walter's little sister.

Chapter Sixteen

November 2, 1879 -- Monterey

Sunday services at the Cathedral of San Carlos Borromeo were always well attended by the Catholic community of Monterey, and that November 2nd was no exception.

Formerly the Royal Presidio Chapel, it was an impressive sandstone structure, dating back to 1795, making it the oldest stone building in California, the oldest parish church in the state, and the last standing reminder of the original Spanish Presidio of Monterey that once dominated the city.

Mass was conducted by Father Lucien du Montfort, an affable Breton Franciscan friar and one-time missionary, who had been appointed the parish priest of Monterey in 1870.

Father Lucien was a natural public speaker, who enjoyed using his pulpit to try and educate his congregation, not unlike a university lecturer, which he had once been, during his many-faceted career with the Franciscan order.

He conducted services twice every Sunday, the first in Spanish, then again in English, along with the liturgy in Latin. Speaking both English and Spanish had been a requirement for his appointment to Monterey, which were only two of the languages Father Lucien had acquired over the years.

Sean and Michael attended the second service, along with Roberto, Katy, and Olivia Connolly.

Michael usually felt a peace listening to the liturgy, and often said a silent confession concerning his activities as a fake Franciscan. Sean might have been able to justify it as bringing comfort to those too far in the wilderness to attend a proper Catholic service, but Michael had his doubts, and even though he never actually confessed this to a priest, confessing it privately to God in a church seemed close enough.

Sean also appeared contemplative during the service, which Olivia interpreted as religious devotion that seemed to belie his otherwise cavalier nature. She found that endearing. It reminded her of her late husband.

Truth was, whenever Sean was able to attend a Mass, he usually took the opportunity to observe the priest's style and technique, to see if there was anything he might incorporate into Father Seamus's performance.

Afterwards, Roberto introduced his old friends to the elderly Franciscan.

"Welcome to Monterey," Father Lucien said, in his Breton accent, which was a mix of French and Breton Celtic.

"Thank you, Father," Michael replied.

"This is a magnificent cathedral," Sean said.

"Named by Father Junípero Serra after Cardinal Carlo Borromeo, the former Archbishop of Milan and a leading figure in the Counter-Reformation."

Sean nodded. He had no idea what the Counter-Reformation was, but it seemed important to Father Lucien.

"We were going to have lunch," Roberto said. "Would you like to join us, Padre?"

"Well, as it happens, my housekeeper is away visiting relatives, so yes, I would very much like to join you."

Even if his housekeeper had been in town, Father Lucien would have accepted the invitation. He took advantage of any opportunity to share a meal and dominate the conversation.

"I have been in Monterey almost ten years. That is the longest I have lived anywhere, since I was boy in Brittany -- almost."

"The Franciscans keep ya movin' about, do they?" Sean asked.

"The days of living behind the walls of a priory are long gone. In my time, I have been a carpenter, scholar, missionary, university professor, and now a parish priest -- continuing the work of Father Serra, bringing the word of God to California."

"And before that," Roberto added, having heard the story a hundred times, "he was a soldier."

"Really?" Sean said.

Father Lucien chuckled. "While I was attending the Sorbonne, I spent part of my time on the barricades in Paris during the February Revolution of 1832. My family, even though we are descended from Breton nobility -- or so I was told -- were fervent republicans. Father died at Waterloo fighting for Napoleon. *Liberté, égalité, fraternité,*" he said, proudly -- then smiled, mischievously. "In all honesty, I only joined the Revolution to meet women. That was before I became a Franciscan, of course."

"Of course," Michael repeated.

"My family never liked the French monarchy," Father Lucien continued. "They have always been coming up with ways to oppress the cultural identities of the different regions of France. In Brittany, they passed a law forbidding the teaching of Breton in the schools. How did it go? *Il est interdit de parler Breton et de cracher par terre*, which means 'it is forbidden to speak Breton at school and to spit on the floor'."

Everyone laughed at the expression. Father Lucien was on a roll.

"What made ya join the church," Sean said. "If ya don't mind my askin'."

"When the Revolution failed, I had to leave Paris quickly. I could not return to Brittany -- for reasons too numerous to go into here -- so I traveled to Italy, with the intention of continuing my education."

"What did you study?" Sean asked.

"Engineering. I always wanted to build things. But I also had a professor of philosophy, who was a Franciscan. He was a great influence on me."

"He must've been," Sean said.

"They didn't have women in Italy?" Roberto asked.

"Oh, yes. Beautiful women. But once I put on the habit and cowl, there was no going back."

Michael and Sean looked at each other, then took a bite to cover up their reaction to Father Lucien's last comment.

After lunch, Michael decided to take a long walk along the peninsula west of town. He wanted to be alone with his thoughts, and, perhaps, get in a little target practice.

As he approached the lighthouse at Point Pinos, he came across a pale young man with long black hair and a stringy mustache, sitting on a tree stump, writing in a notebook.

"Good day," Michael said, as he passed by.

"Good day to you, sir," the young man replied, in an educated Scottish accent. "Beautiful day for a walk, isn't it?"

"Aye, so i' tis."

"I recommend visiting the lighthouse."

"Oh?"

"It's a lovely structure. Well made. Should last for generations."

"Sounds like ya know somethin' about lighthouses."

"It's the family business. My father designs lighthouses, as did his father before him. And now so do my two brothers."

"An' is that what you do?" Michael asked.

"No. I'm a writer." The young man stood up and extended his hand. "Stevenson. Robert Louis Stevenson."

"Michael Lonergan."

"Have you been in Monterey long?"

"Got here yesterday. You?"

"About a month. I've been taking in the sites of Monterey Bay. It's very inspirational."

Michael looked around. "End of the earth. Almost mystical."

"Did you know pirates attacked this place some sixty years ago?"

"Do ya write about pirates then?"

Robert shrugged. "Perhaps. It's an idea."

The two men began to walk toward the lighthouse.

"And what do you do, Mr. Lonergan?"

"Michael." He thought for a moment, then removed his spectacles to wipe off the smudges. "I guess ya could say I observe."

"And what do you observe?"

He returned his spectacles to his face, then lifted the leather loop off the hammer of his gun.

"Mostly, Robert, who needs to be shot."

Before Robert could react to such a statement, Michael drew his Colt revolver and fired off three rounds at a tree, hitting it dead center.

"But, lately, I've been thinkin' o' changin' professions. Explorin' new worlds, more peaceful worlds."

Robert smiled. "Samhain."

"What do you know about Samhain?"

"I'm a Scot."

"Your burr gives ya away."

"As does your brogue."

Michael smiled.

Robert looked down at the Colt. "Can you teach me how to use that?"

"All ya have to do is draw back the hammer an' squeeze the trigger."

Michael twirled the revolver on his finger, then spun it in his palm to present the handle to his new friend.

"The rest just takes practice."

Robert nodded, with a smile, as he took hold of the gun.

After lunch, Sean escorted Olivia back to her ranch in her buggy, with his horse tied to the back for his return trip. She didn't really need an escort. Olivia drove that route almost every day by herself. But she enjoyed being treated like a lady. It was almost as if they were dating.

After about thirty minutes, they came over a ridge, and a well-maintained ranch could be seen spread out before them.

"Beautiful," Sean said.

Olivia smiled, as she often did, when she returned home and got a full view of her estate.

The property was good-sized, by Sean's estimation, and laid out methodically, with a river cutting through the middle of it, and a lake situated not far from the stone and wooden main house, set apart from the two barns, and a bunkhouse for the few ranch hands. There was extensive pasture land for cattle and horses to graze, several acres of recently harvested wheat, and the biggest garden he'd ever seen, with enough fruits and vegetables planted in straight rows to feed a good sized village.

"I acquired it in a mortgage default," she told him. "Then I sold almost half the land to pay for much needed renovations, such as the demolition of the old main house and the building of a new one, more to my liking."

"Very smart." Sean said. Though he never had much money himself, he could appreciate a sound investment.

He even approved of the name she had given the ranch, engraved on the wooden gateway at the property's entrance.

"Loch Éirne. Nice to see a bit o' Ireland so far from Eire."

"My mother was from County Fermanagh. She used to tell me about the two Loch Éirne, when I was a little girl."

As they drove the buggy closer to the main house, they noticed two men sitting on the edge of the lake, with fishing poles in their hands.

"My brother, Liam, and my son, George," Olivia said, by way of introduction, as they drove up. "Neither of them attend church as often as they should."

"We wanted to catch something for dinner," Liam said.

"Any success?" Sean asked.

"Not yet," George replied. "That's why we had to miss church."

"Don't be blasphemous, George," Olivia reprimanded, then gestured to the fellow seated beside her in the buggy. "This is Sean Mulcahy."

George followed the buggy over to the large corral, where he unhitched the horse, while Sean helped Olivia down from the passenger seat.

"Fine horses," Sean observed. "Do ya buy an' sell 'em?"

"For the present, we're breeding them," Olivia said, "to increase our stock."

Sean nodded. "Always investin' in tomorrow."

The lady smiled. "Always."

"Horses, cattle, land," George added.

"Especially land," Olivia said. "Land is the future. Always has been. Always will be."

"Ya just gotta know what land to buy," Sean reasoned.

"That's why California won't let the Chinks own property, even that rundown excuse for a fishing village," George said, then added with a laugh; "But we can!"

"Ya own the Chinese fishin' village?"

"We do now!" George exclaimed, then slapped the buggy horse into the corral with the other horses.

Olivia dropped her smile. "My son has never known when to keep quiet."

"Not to worry," Sean said, reassuring her. "I can keep a confidence as well as any friar, monk, or priest."

Olivia smiled. "As my sainted mother used to tell me, 'We Irish have to stick together'."

"An' that's how we've survived to this day and the next," Sean added, as he held out his arm for her to take.

Olivia proceeded to give her guest a tour of Loch Éirne, while George went back to fishing with his uncle.

.

When Sean returned to the French Hotel, he knocked on Michael's door across the hall from his.

"Come in!"

Sean did, with a smug, self-satisfying expression on his face.

Michael knew that look. "What're ya up to, Seamus?"

Sean poured himself a glass of whiskey from a bottle Michael had on his table.

"The great thing about becomin' friends with the rich is ya sometimes learn some of their dirty secrets, which ya can sometimes use to your advantage."

Michael set down the book he was reading and poured himself a glass as well.

"An' I thought ya liked Olivia."

"Oh, I do, Michaleen. I do. More than ya know."

Then Sean raised his glass. "To quote the lady, 'We Irish have to stick together'."

Michael smiled. "I'll drink to that."

And so they did.

Chapter Seventeen

November 3, 1879 -- Monterey

Michael spent Monday roaming around Monterey, doing a little sightseeing, getting a better feel for the community. He still had a hankering to stay in one place for the winter, and Monterey seemed like as good a place as any.

His first stop was Lau's store. He wanted to know how the little sprite was doing.

Master Lau greeted him at the main counter and reassured him that Shushu was fine. "She in back, working. Hard worker. All Chinese children learn to work hard."

Michael nodded. He would have preferred to see her, but didn't press it.

"You good friends with the marshal?" Lau asked.

"Old friends."

"He know any more about what happened to the Zhangs?"

"Hasn't said anything to me about it."

Master Lau nodded.

Michael began to get distracted by the sound of activity in the back room.

"You like to try your luck?" Lau asked.

"Well, I must confess I was intrigued by the bean game."

The other players found the appearance of a white man in the room a little strange, but he seemed harmless enough, especially as Master Lau had escorted him in.

Michael stood at the *fan-tan* table and watched, as the other players made their bets. One, two, and three seemed to be heavily favored by the other players, so Michael decided to play a hunch and bet on four.

The *tan kun*, the croupier, removed the bowl that had covered the pile of beans and began to flick his bamboo stick, cutting into the pile, always four at a time, until four or less beans remained.

The players were lively and vocal, as they cried out and flailed their arms, certain they had picked the right number. Their enthusiasm was infectious, and Michael spent as much time watching them than he did the pile of beans dwindle.

Finally, the *tan kun* knocked the pile down to five -- then, with one last flick of his wrist, one bean remained.

Michael decided to try four again. Again, the *tan kun* worked his bamboo stick with precision, whittling down the count, until three beans remained.

"Better luck next time, Mr. Lonergan."

Michael turned to find Ying standing in the doorway between the store and the gambling room.

"I'm thinkin', if I keep bettin' on four, I'm bound to win, eventually."

Ying nodded. "Good luck with that."

Michael decided not to place another bet. Instead, he walked over to Ying, who was holding a piece of pastry, wrapped in paper.

"Then again -- maybe I'll stick to poker."

"Mrs. Fuentes asked me to pick up her laundry from down the street, and I had a craving for a piece of Chinese sponge cake. Madame Lau used to make the most wonderful paper wrapped cake. Now she has a baker make the sweets for the store. But they are still good."

Ying tore off a corner of the cake and offered it to Michael.

"This is good," he said. "Can I buy ya another one?"

Ying nodded, with a discreet hint of a smile.

"Then, perhaps, I can help ya carry the laundry home."

Michael bought two more pieces of sponge cake from Master Lau, then the couple stepped outside. Michael took one last look back in through the front window, hoping Shushu might show her face in the shop.

"Do they have cake like this in Ireland?" Ying asked.

"Not that I remember," he replied. "Then again, I'm not sure what I remember about Ireland is the way it was, or just how I choose to remember it."

Ying thought for a moment. "I remember the stories my father used to tell me, when I was a girl."

The couple started walking down the sidewalk to the laundry.

"Like what?"

"Well, there is a legend of an ancient sailor, Hui Shen, a Buddhist monk, who may have discovered California a thousand years before the Spanish."

"He sailed the Pacific over a thousand years ago?"

"He came across on the *Wei Lu*."

"What was that, his ship?"

"No. The *Wei Lu* is the black current that draws ships east across the Pacific."

"The *Wei Lu*," Michael repeated.

"The *Wei Lu* is well known in China. And when Hui Shen finally returned, he told of a place he called Fusang."

"An' that's suppose to be California?"

"Perhaps." Then Ying added, "Do you not believe in legends?"

"Some," Michael said. "There's a legend that an Irish monk, named Brendan, came to America a thousand years before Columbus."

"Who?"

"About the same time as your fellow."

Ying collected the neatly, paper-wrapped clothes from the Chinese laundry, then handed them to Michael to carry, the way she had seen Roberto do with Katy.

"So, Ying. What's your last name?"

"I don't use a last name any more," she stated. "I have had four already. None of them lasted long."

"Four?"

"I came to America with my first husband. He came to work on the railroad. The railroad people came to China to recruit workers back then."

"Really?"

"He worked very hard, but he got sick, when they were laying the track through the mountains -- and he died."

"I'm sorry."

"Then I married a second time -- to another worker on the railroad. He had been a good friend of my first husband's. I was told he died in an avalanche. My third husband was more careful. He was very skilled. He was on a demolition crew. They blew holes in the mountains for the train track to pass through."

"I think I see where this is going," Michael said, trying to add a bit of levity to her sad tale.

"Including the name I was born with," Ying said, "that makes four."

"It's a good thing we didn't meet, when I was workin' on the Union Pacific."

Ying gave him a knowing look.

This was as close as she had been to being courted in years, and the first time by someone not Chinese. It was a new experience for her. She liked it.

Despite Master Lau's reassurances to Michael, Shushu was miserable.

Master Lau was angry that he had to shut down the store in the fishing village, since he no longer had anyone to run it for him, and, for some reason, he seemed to take it out on the little girl. And Madame Lau resented having another mouth to feed, a mouth that, in her opinion, was unable to earn her keep.

Madame Lau asked around if any of the families in Chinatown might have a son that could use a future bride and take Shushu off their hands, but there were no takers.

So, she began to assign Shushu tasks that would be difficult for a girl twice her size, and when she failed, Madame Lau struck her with a switch, telling her how worthless she was.

The second night she was with them, Madame Lau ordered the little girl to rub her tired feet, which Shushu truly detested. The old woman's feet were coarse and smelled like rotting fish. And no matter how Shushu rubbed them, a chore so awful even the Zhangs or her parents back in China had never asked her to do, Madame Lau barked at her, telling her she was doing it wrong.

"I don't know why we took you in," she told the little girl. "My husband is too soft-hearted. If it were up to me, I would throw you out to fend for yourself."

To Shushu, that didn't sound like such a bad idea.

Monday night, right before dinner, Madame Lau sent Shushu on an errand, to deliver a package to a customer down the street. She delivered the package as she was told, then kept on walking, all the way to the Chinese fishing village at Point Alones and the store, where she had lived with the Zhangs. It was locked up, as she expected. Master Lau had put a padlock on the doors to prevent thieves from getting in and stealing anything, until he could figure out what to do with the place.

Shushu had made a few friends among the children in the village, and hoped they might be able to help her. But all they could do was smuggle her a little food and suggest she spend the night under one of the fishing boats that had been pulled ashore and turned upside down to dry off.

Poor Shushu spent the night curled up under a fishing boat, cold and lonely, without a clue of what to do next.

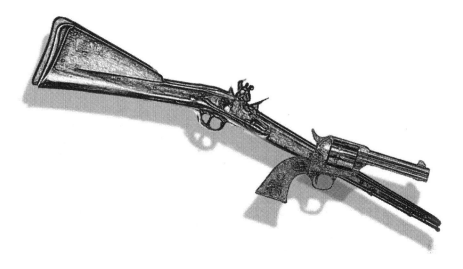

Chapter Eighteen

1848 -- Mexico

Michael finally got a letter stating that he had been honorably discharged from the Mexican Army and a piece of land had been issued in the names of Michael Lonergan and Sean Mulcahy, who had received his honorable discharge from an officer connected with the military hospital.

Their property was on a plain better suited to grazing cattle or horses, and neither one of them knew the first thing about farming, but they decided to try their best.

They bought some seed and planted potatoes, tomatoes, and corn, then, while they waited for their crops to grow, they attempted to build a house. It was a mess -- and never got any better, no matter how hard they worked on it.

As the days wore on, Sean grew ever more restless. For the first time in his life, he was a man of property, but it was fast losing its allure.

"What d'ya think, Michaleen. Fancy a trip to the Pacific?"

"The Pacific?"

"There are a great many cantinas along the coast we could visit."

"Maybe I should stay here an' watch the place," Michael replied.

"Watch it do what? Come on, Michaleen. We could both do with the smell of sea air in our nostrils. Not to mention a little wine an' women."

Michael nodded. He really didn't need that much convincing. "An' two people shorten the road."

Sean smiled, broadly. "Brilliant!"

They purchased their first horses from an obliging neighbor, then quickly realized, once mounted, they didn't have the first clue on how to ride. They bounced comically in the old leather saddles to the amusement of the neighbor's children, as the animals trotted around the farmyard.

Finally, the neighbor took pity on the two army heroes and had his eldest son demonstrate proper technique on another horse, showing them the difference between riding a horse and just sitting on it. It took a while, most of the afternoon, in fact, but by dusk, Sean and Michael at least looked comfortable in the saddle, whether their horses were walking, trotting, or at the gallop. Their backs and backsides were sore, but their spirits were high.

Their visit to the Pacific coast was a success and only encouraged them to give into their Irish wanderlust.

The two men traveled widely along western Mexico, trying their hands at being ranch hands, prospectors, and gamblers, and romancing pretty señoritas and the occasional señoras, when their husbands were away.

The 'D' on Sean's face could usually be counted on for the occasional free drink in a friendly cantina, though, as the years passed, more and more people seemed to forget the old war.

In 1861, French troops began to arrive, taking advantage of the un-united United States to try and turn Mexico into a French colony.

Sean suggested they head north to the American western frontier.

Michael was reluctant.

"The Americans consider us deserters," he cautioned.

"You afraid of bein' branded, Michaleen?" Sean asked.

"The thought's crossed my mind."

Sean smiled. "Not to worry, my friend. America's in the middle of a civil war. Half the country has deserted the other half. I doubt most of 'em even remember there'd been a war in Mexico."

Michael still resisted.

"Then again," Sean suggested, "we could always rejoin the Mexican Army an' fight the French. With our records, they'd probably make us officers."

Michael stared blankly at his friend. "I'd rather go to America."

Sean smiled. That was the response he was hoping for.

The two men rode through the inhospitable Mexican desert, regularly glancing over their shoulders for any signs of Apaches, Yanquis, or bandits that moved through the sparsely populated terrain, while also looking around for any desert animals that might lead them to a hidden waterhole.

A week into their journey, a dozen or so riders began to appear on the ridge off to their left. They weren't very subtle, putting themselves in full view of the two travelers.

"Bandits?" Michael asked, rhetorically.

Sean nodded. "Ya wouldn't think they'd need that many just to rob the two of us, now would ya."

"Does seem like they're hedgin' their bets a might," Michael added.

"Out-numbered. Out-gunned. Looks to me, Michaleen, like our only advantage at the moment is distance."

Michael nodded. "I agree."

Both men jabbed their heels into their horses' flanks, then snapped the reins with a loud "YAH" to get the animals to take off at the gallop.

The bandits took the hint and quickly made their way down the side of the ridge in order to give chase.

Over the years, Sean and Michael had become better and better horsemen, but the bandits rode like they had been born in the saddle. They also had the advantage of knowing the terrain.

The two men ran their horses full out, across the sandy, uneven ground, over and around patches of sagebrush, while the bandits carefully avoided the soft surfaces in any arroyos they came across, which the two Irishmen ruefully discovered slowed them down.

Sean and Michael realized they weren't going to outrun the bandits. Their horses were already foaming all over, sweating profusely. It was only a matter of time before they gave out.

The bandits continued to narrow the gap, with an irritating consistency.

The two men entered a valley, where they were confronted with a collection of earthworks -- or, rather, the remains of man-made earthworks that were eroding away.

"Is it my imagination," Sean said, trying to catch his breath, "or does this place look familiar?"

Michael looked around. "This is where we regrouped after Monterrey." He pointed up, off to his right, at a ridge. "That's where we had our cannons. An' where I caught the grape in my back. Wouldn't be a bad defensive position to fight off the bandits."

Sean was not convinced. "It'd take too long to get up there, Michaleen. They'll be here any minute."

The two looked around.

"How 'bout where the Americans placed their cannons?" Sean suggested.

Michael nodded in agreement.

They rode up to an elevated area across the valley from the much higher ridge they had occupied some fourteen years earlier, tied up their horses behind a rock and dirt wall and positioned themselves behind what was left of the defenses the American riflemen had used to support the cannons.

Sean loaded his army surplus Brown Bess musket, though he used less gunpowder than he did in the Mexican Army, so he could place the butt of the musket against his shoulder for better accuracy, while Michael checked his two revolvers, the old lever-action Colt he had picked up at Churubusco, which he kept in his saddlebag, and a newer Colt Walker, which he was becoming ever more accurate at using.

The bandits took their time riding into the valley. They correctly assumed their targets' horses were on their last legs, and the two men would be on foot. What they weren't sure of was what the pair might do next.

"Hello!" one of the bandits, probably their leader, called out in Spanish. "Are you hiding from us? Why? We don't wish to harm you!"

"That's very nice of them," Sean whispered, reverting to his battlefield blarney to cover his concern over the number of bandits facing them.

"I'm still gonna shoot him," Michael whispered back, matching blarney for blarney with his friend from Cork, which was quite impressive for a lad from Donegal.

"I certainly hope so," Sean answered back.

"Soon as he gets a little closer."

"Not too close."

"No. Not too close."

The bandits fanned out carefully, looking for hoof prints in the ground, to give them an idea which direction the two men might have headed.

While the two Irishmen concentrated on the ever-encroaching bandits, an ominous sound began to divert their attention. It was the rattle of a nearby rattlesnake.

"Bloody hell!" Sean whispered.

The pair began to glance quickly to their left and right, while trying their best to keep their primary attention on the bandits.

"Do ya see it?" Michael whispered.

"No," Sean whispered back. "You?"

"No."

"Keep lookin'," Sean told him. "I'll keep an eye on the bandits."

Michael continued to look all around.

"Shneaky shnaaake," he muttered, angrily. "Where are ya?"

Finally, the venomous serpent made its appearance, slowly winding its way from under some brush toward the two men.

"Gotcha," he whispered, as he pointed his Colt at it.

"Don't shoot," Sean warned him. "You'll give away our position to the bandits."

"I'd rather take a bullet than be bit by a rattler," Michael declared, resolutely.

"Really?" Sean replied.

"Wouldn't you?"

Sean scowled. "If I had my choice, I'd rather not have either."

Michael kept watching the rattler, as it crept ever closer, while sneaking the occasional peek to see what the bandits were up to.

Finally, one of the bandits pointed off in Sean and Michael's direction, without actually seeing them.

"They went that way!" he called out in Spanish.

"Bloody hell," Sean said. "Doesn't he know it's impolite to point?"

"No manners 't all," Michael said, then added, "Can I shoot the bloody viper now?"

"Not yet."

The two men continued to crouch behind the earthwork, peering through some sagebrush they had placed on top of the dirt mound for camouflage, waiting for the bandits to get close enough for their shots to count.

Finally, Sean nodded to his friend. "Now. Shoot it."

Michael didn't have to take aim. He'd already done that, and adjusted it as the accursed sidewinder slid ever closer. With both eyes on the viper, he gently squeezed the trigger. The rattlesnake never knew what hit it.

Sean fired his musket and struck the bandit who had pointed in their direction, while Michael spun around and fired his Colt Walker revolver, shooting the bandit leader, the one who had called out to them in Spanish.

"I was closer to center than you were, Michaleen," Sean said, as he quickly reloaded the musket, using the ramrod to tamp a new the projectile down the muzzle.

"I'll take better aim this time," Michael said, as he fired off another round.

The bandits may have been better horsemen, but the two army-trained veterans were much better shots. While the bandits fired wildly, remaining on their unsteady horses, Sean and Michael took careful aim and, most often, hit their targets.

Eventually, the bandits began to spread out, moving to the left and right of the earthwork.

"They're tryin' to flank us," Sean observed.

"We let 'em spread out," Michael said. "Shoulda kept 'em bunched up."

"Next time, Michaleen. Next time."

Sean raised the musket and took aim at the bandit furthest to his right, when another one succeeded in hitting the Irishman in the arm.

"Damn it to bloody hell!" Sean cried out.

Michael wheeled around and fired twice at the bandit who had shot Sean, hitting him on the second try.

"You all right?" Michael asked.

"No! I'm not all right!"

"I mean, can ya still shoot?"

"Of course I can still shoot!" Sean snapped as he tied a bandana around his arm to stop the bleeding.

Just askin'" Michael said.

"Well, I'm not about to give up!" he snarled.

"Well, I should hope not!"

Sean pulled his handgun, an 1850 Colt .44, and squeezed off a round.

Another bandit fired back, and the bullet struck the earthwork in front of Michael, throwing dirt up into his face.

"Damn!" Michael exclaimed.

As he tried to wipe away the dirt from his eyes, another bullet, hitting the brim of his hat, not only took his hat away, but creased his temple in the process.

"Jesus, Mary, and Joseph," Michael howled, "that does it!"

He emptied his lever-action Colt, firing to his left and right, then quickly reloaded the Colt Walker and fired at one bandit after another.

They were both too mad to be afraid. Michael fired off his six rounds, then reloaded, while Sean fired his .44, keeping up their attack, without stopping.

The wounded bandit leader got back on his horse and tried to rally his men to move in on the two. He seemed to be just as angry as Sean and Michael -- at least until Sean shot him through the heart.

The loss of their leader seemed to knock the spirit out of the bandits.

One of the remaining fellows looked at the number of his comrades now dead on the ground all around him.

"These two aren't worth it anymore!" the fellow called out in Spanish.

The other thieves reluctantly and not so reluctantly agreed. They drew their horses around to make an inglorious escape from the valley, leaving their dead behind.

Michael poured some water from his canteen into his hand to wipe the rest of the dirt from around his eyes.

"Well, you've been thinkin' about gettin' some spectacles for some time, Michaleen," Sean said.

"So I can see better," Michael said. "Not to keep the dirt out o' me eyes."

"So, they'll do both."

"What's the point o' wearin' spectacles, if I always have to be cleanin' 'em?"

Michael ripped away Sean's shirt sleeve to examine his friend's arm wound.

"You're lucky," Michael told him.

"How am I bloody lucky?" Sean wondered aloud.

"The bullet passed clean through. I won't have to dig it out with my dull, dirty pocket knife."

"Well, that's a blessing. Bloody, bleedin', lucky me!"

Michael pulled the cork out of his whiskey bottle with his teeth, poured some into the holes on both sides of Sean's arm, before handing the bottle to his screaming friend, while he removed his own bandana to use as a tourniquet.

Sean took a long drink of whiskey, sighed deeply, and then took another mouthful, before he looked out at the fallen bandits.

"I suppose we're obliged to bury the bastards."

"They wouldn't have buried us," Michael said.

"Which makes us the better Christians," Sean reasoned.

"But, first, we're gonna go through their pockets to see what they got," Michael said.

"Oh, yeah, No point buryin' 'em with full pockets."

"An' we can't leave their horses out here to die in the desert," Michael added.

Sean nodded in agreement. "Wouldn't be Christian."

As they rose to get on with it, Sean grabbed his wounded arm and said, "Ah! You do the buryin.' I'll say the words over 'em."

"Some guys have all the luck."

Sean had been right about the Americans. The people north of the border were much too concerned with the battles being fought between the North and South to be interested in a couple of itinerate Irishmen.

As they made their way onto the great plains, they came across a massive construction project, the transcontinental railroad, being built for the most part by Irish immigrant laborers.

The pay wasn't great, and the work was hard, but being around a host of brogue-speaking fellow refugees from Erin was incentive enough for Sean and Michael to sign on for a while.

The work proved especially hard for Sean, with his bad hip, but having had a bit of an education back in Cork, he quickly wrangled himself an office job, shuffling papers, maintaining employee rosters, and later got himself and Michael onto one of the surveying teams the Union Pacific Railroad employed to make sure they were following the right track toward Utah.

After their time on the railroad, the two men did some mining for silver in New Mexico, but didn't find much. They did learn that an awful lot of miners were terrible poker players, something Sean and Michael had learned to play while in both the American and Mexican Armies and had gotten quite good at, as time went by. They quickly realized there was more money to be made playing poker, than digging for silver.

Sean also noticed a lack of regular religious services in the mining camps.

"Seems a shame the Catholic miners don't have a chance to attend Mass out here," he said.

"The nearest church is just too far away, I suppose," Michael said.

"Maybe the church should come to them," Sean said, with a smile.

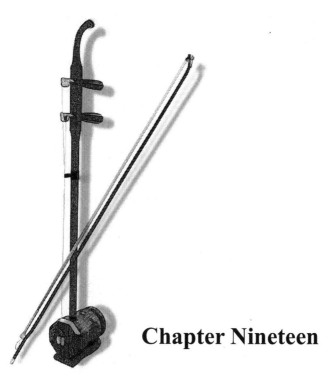

Chapter Nineteen

November 4, 1879 -- Monterey

On Tuesday morning, Father Lucien got up early, made himself some porridge, then got into his carriage and rode out of Monterey to the mission ruins south of town, which was also named after San Carlos Borromeo by Father Serra back in 1770.

The old mission, situated along the Carmel River, held a special place in Father Lucien's heart. The former engineering student had made it his mission to see it rebuilt to its former glory, but had so far only raised enough money to repair the sacristy and put a roof on it.

But it was a start, and the good Franciscan wanted to encourage more contributions. So he held a service at the mission on Tuesday, November 4th, to commemorate the veneration day of San Carlos in the sacristy.

Sean had mixed feelings about attending another service only two days after his last. Religion was fine and even helpful to hone his performance as Father Seamus, but too much religion could cut into his time courting Olivia or his poker playing, his preferred activity when Olivia was working at the bank.

But he kept those feelings to himself, since Olivia had expressed an interest in attending the service, and he liked proving to her what a sincere Catholic he was, which seemed to have a favorable impression on her.

Olivia's own motive for attending the Mass was more economic. She had passed by the old ruins on several occasions and considered making a suggestion to the county to have it torn down. But it was owned by the Church, beyond their control.

Now, with the plans to make Monterey a tourist attraction, the historical significance of the mission seemed to be worth investigating as another tourist site, another reason to visit Monterey.

Michael also attended the service, escorting Katy Fuentes, as Roberto had to work. And they gave a ride to the Scotsman, Robert Louis Stevenson, who they came across, walking toward the Mission.

The majority of the congregation was made up of members of the Rumsen tribe, or, as Katy explained, the last of the Rumsen tribe that once populated the Monterey shoreline. These were the descendants of the men and women who had been converted to Christianity by Father Serra and his fellow Franciscan missionaries and had helped build the mission.

Even the choir was made up of tribal members, under the direction of a blind old man. Sean and Michael were impressed by how well they sang in Latin, even if it did ring heavily with what must have been a Rumsen accent to the enunciation. Despite all the misery the Europeans had heaped upon this ever dwindling tribe, they still showed a joy in their worship of God.

It even impressed Stevenson, who quietly confessed to Michael that he was a confirmed atheist.

After the service, Father Lucien gave Sean, Olivia, Michael, Katy, and Stevenson the ten cent tour, starting with the roofless basilica.

"This was the second mission founded by Father Junípero Serra, and it became his headquarters. After he died, his successor brought in stonemasons to build the structure you see today."

Slowly, he led the group through the large, open room.

"When the Mexican government secularized the California missions in 1833, the local rancheros laid claim to much of the grazing and farm land, but did not spend any time or money keeping up repairs on the churches."

Father Lucien looked around the basilica, seeing in his mind's eye how it used to look -- and could look again.

"This was Father Serra's favorite of all the missions that he built up and down the California coast. He died here in 1784 and was buried in the Chapel of the Blessed Sacrament, over there." He gestured to what was left of a small altar and a concrete tomb. "There were rumors that his body was moved after the secularization of the mission, but I believe he is still here, still looking after his favorite mission. It is my wish to restore the mission by 1884, to commemorate the centennial of his passing, beginning with the rebuilding of the roof."

Olivia also had visions of how wonderful the mission church could look, with new pews, the intricate woodwork restored, and the brilliantly colored artistry on the wall behind the altar reimagined.

"It would be a real piece of California history come back to life," she said. "And only a short distance from Monterey."

"That was on purpose," Father Lucien told her. "The original mission was built as part of the Presidio of Monterey, but Father Serra had a falling out with the Presidio's military commander, so he moved the mission here, and the original mission structure became the Presidio's church, which is why both are named after San Carlos de Borromeo."

"What would it take to rebuild the mission, Father?" Olivia asked.

"Oh, I think a little faith, some carpenters, stone masons, plasterers, artisans -- and money."

Olivia smiled. "Of course."

Sean looked around. "Probably a whole lot o' faith, Father."

Father Lucien smiled. "Well, perhaps a little faith from a whole lot of people."

After the tour, Sean took Olivia on an extended buggy ride along Point Pinos, overlooking the Pacific.

"It's spectacular," Sean exclaimed. "A view worth the trip from any distance."

"I certainly hope so," Olivia said. "We intend to make Monterey a first class destination."

"An' then what?"

"And then what -- what?"

"After you've made a pot full o' money, how do ya intend to enjoy it?"

Olivia paused to think. "I don't know. What would you do?"

"I'd travel," Sean said.

"You've been doing that all your life."

117

"Travel around the world in first class luxury. By steam ship, in first class train cabins, at first class hotels. I mean, what's the point o' makin' that much money, if ya don't enjoy spendin' it?"

"But who'll watch over the bank or the ranch?"

"That's why ya have employees," Sean said. "What? Ya think the robber barons that built the railroads don't have dozens o' lawyers an' vice presidents to look after their assets, while they conquer new horizons?"

Olivia loved that Sean had thought to compare her to the visionary builders of the Central Pacific: Crocker, Hopkins, Huntington, and Stanford. Her fortune was nothing compared to theirs, but she felt she could be just as bright, just as strategic, and just as ruthless as they had been in their storied careers.

She liked the better things in life, like imported Waterford Crystal and Wedgwood China -- and staying in first class hotels, when she traveled to San Francisco or Sacramento on business.

As they continued their trip around the Monterey peninsula, they came across a collection of finely built wooden cabins laid out in straight rows along well-marked dirt paths, as neatly as any planned community on the planet.

"That's the Pacific Camp Grounds," Olivia explained. "It's a Christian seaside resort built four years ago by a Methodist couple from Scotland."

"Looks abandoned."

"Closed for the winter. But I understand they do a pretty good business during the summer, advocating prayer, Spartan living, and teetotalism."

"Well," Sean said. "A good tourist location needs to appeal to all types, I suppose. Just how Spartan are the livin' conditions?"

"I don't know," Olivia replied. "I've never been out here before."

Sean tried to look inside one of the cabins, but it was tightly shuttered.

Olivia tried the door, but it was locked.

"Guess they don't want squatters during the winter months," Olivia said.

Sean tried the door to another cabin, then was able to quietly jimmy it open with his pocket knife.

"Looks like they forgot to lock this one." he said.

The cabin was, indeed, Spartan, and yet it had a homey, friendly quality to it all the same.

"At least the mattress is soft," Olivia said, sitting on it.

Sean sat next to her. "I imagine it's tough to concentrate on prayer all day, if ya don't get a good night's sleep."

The two looked at one another, then leaned in for a kiss. And then another.

After the second kiss, Olivia hesitated. She had not been with a man since her husband died several years ago and did not want to go too fast.

Instead, she paused to run her fingers across his scruffy blonde beard, then traced the contours of the 'D' on his right cheek.

"That must have been extremely painful."

"A memento from my days in the army," he replied.

"Did you fight in Mexico?"

Sean nods. "That's where Michael an' I met Roberto."

"I figured as much," Olivia said. "The only time I ever heard of Marshal Fuentes being away from Monterey for any time was when he was in Mexico."

Sean nodded. Like a lot of soldiers through the years, he didn't like talking about the war, unless it might earn him a free drink in Mexico, and then he mostly lied about it.

She brushed his whiskers back over the dead skin. "I also heard about a group of Irishmen who fought for the Mexicans."

Sean hesitated, then said, "The San Patricios."

"That's it. The San Patricios. A number of miners I met through the years, who had fought in the war -- every time they learned I was of Irish descent -- they'd tell me about that 'damned St. Patrick's Battalion'. Apparently, you were extremely accurate with your cannon fire."

Sean remained silent, but let a hint of a smile crease his lips, showing he was still proud of his former unit.

"They told me that several of the deserters were hung, while others were given fifty lashes with a whip, then had the letter 'D' branded on their faces."

"Did they now?"

Olivia paused for a moment, then looked into his eyes.

"So, did all that brutal punishment teach you a lesson about doing the right thing?"

"Not for a moment, Darlin'. Not for a bloody, bleedin' moment."

"Thank goodness. I was afraid maybe it had."

Sean smiled, as Olivia leaned in for another kiss. And then another, before they stretched out onto the bed, cautiously.

Sean had taken the hint. Even though all of his sexual exploits in recent years had been with willing women of easy virtue, living and working above various saloons throughout the western frontier, he could readily sense Olivia's reluctance to hurry anything between them.

But he could also tell she was willing enough, if he was patient and gentle. So, he became the very soul of gentlemanly discretion, which resulted in their spending a most pleasurable afternoon together.

Michael escorted Katy back to the Fuentes home, where Ana cajoled "Uncle Miguelito" into playing a tune on the fiddle.

Afterwards, Katy sent Ying on an errand to the Chinese fishing village to buy some fresh fish for dinner. She also suggested that Michael might like to go along with her, then handed Ying her knit shopping bag, with a smile.

The fishing village was little more than a collection of ramshackle houses and storage sheds right on the shoreline, along with racks covered in gutted fish, drying in the sun. The place reeked of fish, but it felt very nostalgic to Michael.

"All these men used to work on the railroad?" Michael asked.

"No," Ying said. "These are Tanka. Boat people. They live their whole lives on the shore or at sea."

"Sounds like my people back in Donegal. So, what brought 'em to California?"

"The *Wei Lu*."

"Of course."

Michael looked about the village, at the small boats, similar to the ones he knew back in the Ireland, the fishing nets, hanging against the houses, that needed regular mending, and the scores of fish laid out under the sun.

"Why do they put so much fish out to dry?"

"They ship most of their catch to the Chinatown in San Francisco."

"They don't sell it locally?"

"Most white people don't buy fish from Chinese."

"Why not?"

Ying shrugged. "They won't."

Michael thought about that for a moment. "What if the Chinese had a white middle man to sell their fish?"

"You wish to go into the fish business?"

121

Michael shrugged. "I was born in the fish business."

Ying thought about that for a moment.

"I think it's a good idea. I think, maybe, the fishermen will think so, too."

Just then, Michael and Ying began to hear music being played. They followed the sound and found a group of Chinese listening to three musicians playing a flute, a lute, and something akin to a violin, except it only had two strings and was played upright with a bow, almost like a small cello.

The song had a sad, shrill quality to it, especially the music coming from the bamboo flute, while the man playing the cello-like instrument pulled his bow to create a scratch-like sound, and the third man plucked at the lute with what Michael felt were heavy-handed fingers.

"The instrument that man is plucking is called a *pipa*," Ying told him. "The one played with a bow is called an *ehru*. And the flute instrument is called a *dizi*."

After they finished the song and were greeted with warm applause from the crowd, Ying said something to the musicians Michael assumed was a request. The musician playing the cello-like instrument took the lead and broke into a quick-tempo, upbeat song.

Michael was amazed at how familiar the new song sounded to him.

"When did Chinese musicians learn to play Irish music?"

"Maybe the Chinese monk and the Irish monk who both came to America met one another a thousand years ago," Ying suggested.

"Ya mean that's a Chinese song?"

"Has been, for many years."

When the musicians finished. Ying opened the shopping bag and pulled out the Fuentes's fiddle and bow.

122

"A gift from Mrs. Fuentes" she said with a mischievous grin. "Would you like to join them?"

Michael smiled, then tucked the fiddle under his chin and began to play a popular Irish reel.

The crowd was surprised this non-Chinese fellow knew how to play what sounded like a Chinese folk song.

It sounded familiar to the musicians as well, and they began to play along with him.

Michael began to laugh. He hadn't played with another musician since his days in the Mexican Army, and he had forgotten how much fun it could be.

Several members of the crowd asked Ying who the white musician was and how he knew Chinese folk music. She just smiled and said that the Chinese and Irish were alike in many ways.

The music brought out another listener. Shushu heard the fiddle and came out to see if it was who she hoped it was.

It was.

"Yeh Yeh!" she cried out. *"Yeh Yeh!"*

Shushu ran over and hugged Michael around the legs, as he finished the song.

He kneeled down to get a better look at her. "What are you doing here, little sprite?"

She said something in her rapid fire manner, which Ying translated as, "She ran away from the Laus. She hates them. They hate her. So, she ran away. She wants to be with you, Michael. And she calls you *Yeh Yeh.*"

"Yeh Yeh?"

"Grandfather," Ying said. "She is calling you grandfather."

"And why would she be doin' that?"

Ying asked her, and Shushu said it was because his fiddle playing reminded her of her grandfather.

123

"He played an *ehru*," Ying told him, "Like that fellow there. And her grandfather was the last person who was nice to her."

Michael stroked Shushu's hair with his free hand. "Tell her I'm very flattered, but I don't know the first blessed thing about taking care of a little girl."

Shushu didn't like what Ying told her and grabbed Michael even tighter.

"Please do not send me back to the Laus!" Ying translated. "Madame Lau beats me."

Not one for discussing private matters in public, Michael took the little girl by the hand and led her out of view of the crowd, but not before announcing, and Ying translating, that he'd right back and for the other musicians to continue without him.

"Now, what's this about the Laus beatin' her?" he asked Ying, while looking into Shushu's tear-filled eyes.

Shushu turned away from Michael, then pulled up her jacket to show the welts from where Madame Lau had struck her.

"She says I can not do anything right," Ying translated. "That I am worthless."

"Sounds like my old army sergeant."

Michael reached out and gently touched the welts on her back.

"Tell her she doesn't have to go back."

"You are going to adopt her?" Ying asked.

"Well, I can't be sending her back to the Lau's, now, can I?"

Michael pulled up his shirt and showed the two ladies the thirty year old scars that the army whippings and grape shot shrapnel had left on his back.

"I don't like people who beat other people."

Ying winced at the sight of the scars left by the brutality Michael had experienced some thirty years ago, a permanent disfiguration of criss-crossing welts from his shoulders to his belt line.

Shushu reached out and tenderly touched the scars, before he lowered his shirt.

"But first things first," Michael said. "I'm willin' to bet she could do with a really big meal."

Ying translated his observation. Shushu smiled broadly, and nodded her head, enthusiastically.

Michael smiled, as did Ying, even if hers was a little more cautious. She wasn't so sure he knew what he had taken on.

Then again, neither did he.

Chapter Twenty

November 4, 1879 -- Monterey

By Tuesday, it had become apparent to Marshal Fuentes that Sheriff Lang was not interested in who had killed the Zhang family on the dunes south of town. He knew it was out of his jurisdiction. Not only was the crime committed outside of Monterey's city limits, but, since the Zhangs lived in the Point Alones Chinese fishing village, they weren't even residents of Monterey.

Nevertheless, Roberto took his job seriously. He believed in law and order. That's why he ran for the office in the first place. And it galled him that Lang didn't seem to care, just because the victims were Chinese. So, he decided to do a little investigating himself.

He made his way down the main street, visiting one saloon after another, chatting with the bartenders and picking up the latest gossip. Between the sordid details of who was cheating on their wives -- or husbands -- and who seemed to be drinking more than usual or losing more at cards, Roberto heard about a couple young fellows who'd been bragging about some vague anti-Chinese stunt they had committed. The bartender guessed it had been some sort of act of minor vandalism or petty theft against the Chinese at Point Alones.

"These boys are mostly talk," the bartender told Roberto. "They steal some fish or slash a hole in one of the Chinamen's nets, and you'd think they'd won some huge victory against the yellow menace."

The bartender identified the pair as Billy Clark and Carl Morgan. Roberto knew them, two minor miscreants he'd had occasion to lock up overnight for drunk and disorderly, amongst other things. But cold-blooded murder was quite another thing all together. Still, they were his first leads, so Roberto decided to look into them.

When he returned to his office, he found three visitors waiting for him.

"What's the rule in California for adopting a Chinese girl?" Michael asked.

"That depends," Roberto replied. "Do you want to adopt Shushu or Ying?"

"Shushu," Michael answered. Then he looked at Ying. "For starters."

Ying smiled, almost blushing.

"Well, the Chinese have little legal standing in California. They're not allowed to own property. Most of them aren't even citizens. Still, you probably oughta make some sorta deal with the Laus, though I got the impression they weren't all that happy to take her in the first place. Are you sure you want to adopt her?"

Michael nodded at Roberto, then turned and nodded at Shushu, who nodded back at him with a smile.

"Okay then," Roberto said. "First, you should have a contract for Lau to sign." Roberto pulled out a sheet of stationery from his desk with the City of Monterey letterhead emblazoned across the top and began writing.

"Offer them twenty dollars," Ying suggested.

Roberto nodded. "Good idea."

Michael wasn't so sure. "It feels like I'm buyin' Shushu."

"You're not buying Shushu," Roberto countered. "You're buying off the Laus."

"Oh. Okay."

The Laus were both surprised and angry to see Shushu back. As Madame Lau came around the counter to grab the little girl, Marshal Fuentes stepped in front of her.

"Hold on. Mister Lonergan has a proposition," Roberto said.

"Proposition?" asked Master Lau.

"I want to adopt Shushu," Michael said slowly, while Ying translated into Cantonese, so there would be no misunderstanding. "I want you to relinquish all custody to her."

"You can have her," Madame Lau said in Cantonese, with Ying translating. "Ungrateful, willful child."

Roberto and Michael looked at one another, then the marshal crossed out the section on remuneration, before Michael and Master Lau both signed.

"This may be an inopportune moment to ask such a question," Sean said, as he and Olivia rode back to Monterey, after their afternoon in the cabin, "but what kind of collateral does your bank require to take out a loan?"

"That depends," Olivia replied. "What kind of collateral do you have?"

128

"Not much. My horse, my honest face, and a small farm that Michael and I own down in Mexico. At least, I think we still own it. We haven't been back in a few years."

"What were you thinking of doing with this loan?" she asked.

"Buy some land, if there's any left around Monterey to be bought at a cheap price."

"I don't know about a cheap price, but there is still land to be bought, especially out past Point Alones."

"Near the mission? That'd be grand. Maybe lease the property to someone who'd operate a restaurant for people who visit the restin' place of Father Serra -- assumin' Father Lucien gets the roof built on the rest o' the building."

"Then you plan on staying in Monterey for a while?" she asked, half coyly and half as a professional businesswoman.

"Land does have a way of makin' a fella plant roots."

"What about that farm in Mexico? Any roots there?"

"Naw. Michael an' I realized we weren't cut out to be farmers."

"Why didn't you sell it?"

"No one to sell it to. It was just after the war with the United States, an' nobody in Mexico, at least, that part of Mexico, had money to buy anything."

"Well, thanks to my son's big mouth, you know my brother and I have been buying up land in and around the Chinese fishing village, which is perfectly legal. But I would prefer not to advertise these purchases for the present. As a banker, I like to present myself as interested in the well being of all the diverse communities in and around Monterey."

"I would suppose a banker's reputation for honesty an' fairness should be second only to a man o' the cloth," Sean said.

"Exactly," Olivia said. "But if I formed a company, that was separate from the bank, but that I would still control completely, that company would still need another person to serve as its nominal president."

"And what might the salary be for this nominal president, who, of course, would remain completely loyal to his silent partner?"

"Silent *Owner*."

"Silent *Owner*," Sean repeated.

"That's something we could discuss. Of course, the nominal president would have to stay close to Monterey."

Sean smiled. "Of course."

Olivia smiled. She was finding this charming Irishman nice to have around. And yet, part of her wondered just how far he could be trusted with her money. She decided that he would need to prove himself a little more, before she could trust him as a business partner.

When Sean got back to the hotel, he knocked on Michael's door across the hall from his, then, finding the door unlocked, entered, before he was invited.

He found his friend sitting in the darkened room, reading a book by the light of a kerosene lamp.

"Oh, Michaleen. Comin' to Monterey was the best thing we've done in a long time."

"Oh?"

"Olivia is everything I could hope for in a woman -- rich, beautiful, an' not above a little shady dealin' on the side."

Sean caught himself, before he went into any further detail. After all, he had promised to honor her confidences, and Father Seamus never broke a confidence, even to Father Michael.

Just then, Shushu, who was asleep in the bed, made a sound and turned onto her side.

"What's she doin' here?"

"I adopted her," Michael said.

"Adopted her? An' when did this happen?"

"This afternoon."

"What happened to the Laus?"

"They beat her, Sean. I saw the welts."

Sean nodded. He knew his friend's kind-hearted nature all too well.

"Well, she'll make an interestin' travelin' companion for us," Sean said.

"What about your shady deal with Olivia?"

"That should only take a year or so." Sean sat in the second chair, close to his friend. "You know me, Michaleen. I can never stay in one place for long. An' by that time, I'm pretty sure I'll have talked Olivia into doin' some travelin' -- first class, of course."

Michael picked up the bottle of Irish whiskey on the table and poured some into two glasses, then offered one to Sean.

"Well, I'm happy for ya, Seamus. I hope it all works out for you an' Olivia. She'll certainly make a more attractive travelin' companion than I've been."

Michael touched his glass to Sean's.

"I was thinkin' about stayin' here in Monterey anyway, startin' up a business, sellin' fish the Chinese catch to the non-Chinese."

"Really? The Chinese at the fishin' village south of here?"

"Yeah. The whites won't buy from the Chinese -- so I'll act as a sort of middle man -- and they won't have to ship all their fish to San Francisco."

Sean took a sip of whiskey to give himself time to think about what his friend just told him -- and what, if anything, he should or could tell him about Olivia's plans to push the fishermen off Point Alones -- and how that could affect his business plan.

Mixed loyalties were something new to him -- and he definitely didn't like having them.

"I'm also thinkin' of askin' Ying to marry me," Michael said with a smile.

"The Chinese housekeeper?"

"She's rather partial to men who worked on the railroad."

Sean finished off his whiskey.

"She's very attractive, Michaleen, but I'm pretty sure there are miscegenation laws in this state."

Michael poured them both a second round.

"Since when have you been worried about the odd law, Seamus?"

"There's skirtin' the law, boyo, an' there's a blatant disregard for it. You don't want Bob to throw you in jail, do ya?"

"Bob drew up the paper for the Laus to give up their claim on Shushu. An' Katy Fuentes has been encouragin' Ying an' me to spend time together."

"An' what about Sheriff Lang? He seems to be about as anti-Chinese as you can get around these parts. He might just lock you up in the county jail."

Michael patted his friend on the shoulder. "I'll be fine, Seamus."

"So, this is the end of the road for us, then, Michaleen?"

"You won't be goin' anywhere for a while. In the meantime, we can be each other's best man, when we get married."

"Married?"

"You don't think Olivia's gonna travel all around the world with you, if you're not married, do ya, Seamus?"

Sean sighed. He hadn't thought of that. He took another long taste of whiskey, then laughed before launching into a new poem.

"Poor Michaleen an' me, confirmed wanderers, we.
'Til winds of fate brought us to Monterey,
Had hoped to win at poker, but love we didn't broker.
So now it seems we're both inclined to stay."

Shushu made another noise and rolled onto her stomach.

"Makes a lot of noise for someone that small, doesn't she?"

"She's my little sprite," he said with a smile.

"I didn't know Chinese faeries appeared at Samhain."

"I guess ya never know what'll step through the veil."

"Ya know," Sean said. "I don't really believe in all that."

Michael smiled, knowingly.

"That's because you're not from Donegal."

Chapter Twenty-One

November 5, 1879 -- Monterey

Apparently, someone staying at the French Hotel had spread the word that an Irishman staying there had adopted a little Chinese girl who had lived with the family that had been killed on the dunes. People began to wonder why an Irishman, who also happened to be an old friend of the town marshal, would want to adopt a Chinese girl -- and what, if anything, might she have seen, if, in fact, she had been out on the dunes with that Chinese family.

When Billy Clark and Carl Morgan learned about the little girl, they were naturally worried. Had she been out there on the dunes? If she had, why didn't they see her? And just because they hadn't seen her, did she see them?

George Connolly wasn't worried. "She's a kid. A little girl. And Chinese. Can't even speak English. Who's gonna take the word of an ignorant Chinese girl over ours?"

George leaned back confidently. "Nobody cares what happened on the beach. But I wouldn't go around bragging about it anymore."

Billy and Carl agreed, at least on the surface.

After his talk with Michael the night before, Sean had a lot to think about. His life was changing. His relationship with Olivia was becoming complicated, as was his friendship with Michael.

He had sworn to Olivia not to reveal her confidences, but he had never kept a secret from his best friend. And how much about Michael's plans could he tell to Olivia, without breaking faith with his old traveling companion?

"This is what comes from tryin' to be respectable," Sean said to himself.

As he passed by the cathedral, he noticed Father Lucien coming out of the rectory and climbing onto the seat of his one horse buggy.

"Mornin', Father," Sean said.

"Ah, Mulcahy. Good morning to you."

"Off to visit the flock?"

"Actually, I am meeting a potential benefactress, who may wish to help fund the reconstruction of the Mission San Carlos. She came in by train last night from San Francisco. I am meeting her at he mission."

"Well, good luck to ya."

"Why don't you come along?" Father Lucien suggested. "I dislike buggy rides with no one to talk to."

Since Olivia was busy at the bank, and he didn't really like playing poker that early in the day, Sean decided to accept the invitation.

"Why not? As we say in Ireland, two people shorten the road."

"Very good!"

Sean climbed up beside the Franciscan, and Father Lucien gave his horse a snap of the reins.

"So," Father Lucien began. "How do you like Monterey?"

"Oh, it's a grand place, Father."

"Yes," Father Lucien said, knowingly. "I have noticed how you have been spending a good deal of time with the widow Connolly."

"Ya don't approve?"

"Now did I say that? Olivia Connolly is a fine, upstanding member of the community and the Church."

"Ya don't have to worry about me, Father. I'm as harmless as harmless can be."

"Blessed are the meek, for they shall inherit the earth," Father Lucien said, quoting the Gospel of Matthew.

Sean smiled. He knew that passage of The Bible very well and had used it in his sermons on more than one occasion, particularly, if there happened to be women and children in the congregation.

"Blessed are the merciful," Sean answered back, "for they shall obtain mercy."

Father Lucien was pleasantly surprised by Sean's response, then continued with, "Blessed are the pure in heart, for they shall see God."

To which Sean finished with, "Blessed are the peacemakers, for they shall be called the children of God."

"Very good, Mr. Mulcahy," Father Lucien said with a laugh. "Except you skipped over 'Blessed are they which do hunger and thirst after righteousness'."

"So, I did, Father. Then again, I've never been one to judge who is righteous an' who is not."

Father Lucien nodded. "Judge not, that ye not be judged."

"Took the words right out of . . ."

"His mouth."

"Exactly, Father. Exactly."

They both laughed.

"You know, Brother Sean -- you might have made a fine Franciscan," Father Lucien said, making a keen observation.

Sean smiled, knowingly. "As a matter of fact, you're not the first person to think that, Father."

When they arrived at the mission, another buggy was already there, with the hired driver waiting beside the horse.

Father Lucien checked the time on his pocket watch.

"She is early."

"That a good sign -- or bad?" Sean wondered out loud.

Father Lucien and Sean got off the buggy and hurried into the mission's basilica, where they found Mrs. Alice Faulkner looking about in the ruins.

It was apparent from her appearance, her dress, and her manner that Mrs. Faulkner was a highly cultured and a very wealthy woman -- just the kind of person the good padre would need to induce to invest in the mission's reconstruction.

"Mrs. Faulkner," Father Lucien said, as he walked up to her. "I do apologize for keeping you waiting."

The elderly lady checked the watch she kept in a small pocket in her tailored jacket. "No need for an apology, Father. As it happened, I arrived some twenty minutes ahead of our scheduled meeting -- and you are ten minutes early yourself."

The Breton father was unsure how to respond, so he gestured to the smiling fellow next to him. "Sean Mulcahy."

"Mrs. Faulkner," Sean said, nodding politely, but keeping a proper distance.

"Mr. Mulcahy," Mrs. Faulkner answered back.

Father Lucien began his tour of the basilica, almost word for word to the one he had given Sean and the others on Tuesday -- and had many times before that with others. But Mrs. Faulkner remained unimpressed.

"Do you intend to tear down the walls and rebuild?"

"Oh, no," the father replied. "I have had an engineer examine the remaining structure, and he assured me that the walls still standing are in excellent shape."

Mrs. Faulkner looked around, not quite believing it, but said nothing -- so Father Lucien continued.

"The first priority would be to hire a team of carpenters to cut and attach new beams to rebuild the ceiling and enclose the basilica -- then fill in any holes in the walls, re-plaster it all, and give it a fresh coat of white wash. Then we can hire artisans to restore the woodwork on the altar and pulpit and artists for the frescoes on the walls, before they completely fade away."

Mrs. Faulkner nodded. Then, after a long pause, she added, "How much would you need to begin work, Father?"

"Bless you, Mrs. Faulkner," Father Lucien declared, "and all those who hunger and thirst for righteousness."

"Let me be clear, Father," Mrs. Faulkner said, cutting him off. "This donation has nothing to do with a hunger for righteousness. If I go ahead and help fund your resurrection of this building, it is not out of some sense of religious fervor or even guilt. I'm not even Catholic. I'm Episcopalian, and we don't believe in guilt."

Mrs. Faulkner continued to walk around, touching the ceiling beams and broken pews.

"My husband lost his right arm in Mexico, during the war, blown off by cannon fire by some 'damned Irishmen', although what Irishmen were doing fighting for the Mexicans is beyond me."

Sean remained silent.

"Actually, losing his arm was the best thing that could have happened to Rufus. It put the idea of being a career soldier right out of his head, and I was able to get him to concentrate on business. He made a lot of money, and we had a fine life. But Rufus passed away a few years back, and now I'm looking for places to donate my money. I'm getting on in years, and I don't intend to leave all that much to my daughter and that wastrel excuse she chose for a husband."

Mrs. Faulkner turned and crossed back to Sean and Father Lucien for her big finish.

"So, I've become a philanthropist, which gets me invited to all the best parties, which gets me out of the house. Of course, they only invite me for my money, but that's all right. I only go to be flattered and have charming young men ask me to dance."

She looked at Sean with a knowing grin, then walked out of the basilica without another word.

Sean paused, then looked at Father Lucien. "It just seems to get harder an' harder to find someone hungerin' or thirstin' for righteousness these days, Father."

"That's all right," Father Lucien replied. "I'll keep looking."

Michael and Shushu spent the morning buying her a nicer set of clothes, a new pair of shoes, some pocket handkerchiefs, a comb, hair brush, toothbrush, and hair braids. Shushu also found a silly, little, raggedy cloth doll with button eyes that she loved. It immediately became permanently attached to her right hand and, occasionally, her left.

That afternoon, they took a walk out to the edge of town and sat in the shade of one of the dwindling nests of trees that still surrounded Monterey, where Michael read to Shushu from a picture book he'd also purchased that morning. He decided the first thing he needed to do was teach her English. Later, maybe, he'd teach her how to play the fiddle, but English came first.

Shushu took to learning as eagerly as she took to the contents of their picnic basket. Feeding her brain and feeding her stomach were clearly two of her favorite things.

Another example, Michael thought, of what the Irish and the Chinese had in common -- or, at least, what the two of them had in common.

When they returned to the hotel, they found Robert Louis Stevenson sitting on the porch, writing in his notebook.

"Workin' on your pirate story?" Michael asked.

"No," Robert replied, with a smile. "Not yet. I'm trying my hand at a little poetry. I don't think I told you, but I'm on my way to San Francisco to meet my fiancée. My intended fiancée. She hasn't actually accepted my proposal, yet."

"What's stoppin' her?"

"Her present husband. Although they're getting a divorce. Anyway, Fanny has a young son, and I thought I might write some children's poems for him."

"What a wonderful idea," Michael said, as he and Shushu sat on a wicker swing nearby. "Might we hear one?"

"If you'd like." Robert flipped back through his notebook a couple pages. "Here's one I wrote last week." He looked over at Shushu. "Of course, you don't understand English, do you, little one."

"You'd be surprised how fast she's learnin'."

"Good for her," Robert said. "Well, I call this one, 'My Shadow'."

140

Michael looked at Shushu. "Do ya know what a shadow is, little sprite?"

She looked back at him with a questioning stare.

Michael held up her arm, then pointed at the shadow her cloth doll made on the wooden porch beside her.

"That's a shadow," he told her.

"Shadow," she repeated, then moved her doll back and forth to watch her shadow dance. She giggled at her control of this phenomenon of nature.

"Very good," Robert said. Then he dropped his voice in pitch and tone, as he read aloud his poem.

"I have a little shadow that goes in and out with me,
And what can be the use for him is more than I can see.
He is very, very like me from the heels up to the head;
And I see him jump before me, when I jump into my bed."

Shushu did not understand what he said in his velvety Scottish burr, but his delivery was mesmerizing, like listening to a song being spoken to her.

"The funniest thing about him is the way he likes to grow,
Not at all like proper children, which is always very slow;
For he sometimes shoots up taller like an india-rubber ball,
And he sometimes gets so little that there's none of him at all."

Michael found the poem amusing and sweet. He even turned at one point to watch the men and women passing by the hotel, with their long afternoon shadows either preceding or following them without their slightest acknowledgment.

"He hasn't got a notion of how children ought to play,
And can only make a fool of me in every sort of way.
He stays so close beside me, he's a coward you can see;
I'd think shame to stick to nursie as that shadow sticks to me!"

141

For some reason, Shushu chose that exact moment to take Michael's arm and snuggle close to him. He interpreted her gesture as understanding the poem better than either he or Robert could have guessed, patted her hand affectionately, and received a big smile in return.

"One morning, very early, before the sun was up,
I rose and found the shining dew on every buttercup;
But my lazy little shadow, like an arrant sleepy-head,
Had stayed at home behind me and was fast asleep in bed."

When Robert finished, Shushu and Michael applauded, then Michael directed Shushu's attention out at the street to watch the people and their shadows pass by.

Shushu had probably never thought about shadows before that moment, but now it was something new and exciting. Everything had a shadow: people, horses, even buildings.

Her eyes darted about the street, looking at all the shadows caused by the late afternoon sun -- then suddenly stopped, when she caught sight of a young man standing across the street, talking to a young lady.

Shushu recognized the young man. He was one of the men who had killed and robbed the Zhangs, the one in the black hat, which he was still wearing.

Michael didn't notice the change in her behavior. He was too busy talking to Robert about poetry and music. Robert revealed that he also composed music from time to time and loved to play the flageolet, which was a sort of small recorder, and Michael commented that he and Shushu would love to hear him play sometime.

He didn't notice that she was still staring at someone across the street.

But the man in the black hat noticed her.

142

Chapter Twenty-Two

November 6, 1879 -- Monterey

George Connolly had already begun to have second thoughts about what the little Chinese girl might or might not have seen. Maybe it might be best for everyone -- and by everyone, he meant himself -- if the little girl left town.

Unfortunately, Lonergan showed no signs of going anywhere. He and his friend, who had recently taken up with George's mother, were becoming permanent fixtures in the Monterey community.

Then, when George saw how Shushu reacted to seeing him, he knew she had been there, when they killed and robbed the Zhangs. The bluster he had spewed out for Billy and Carl's benefit disappeared. She could identify them. Whether a jury would believe her, or would an anti-Chinese sheriff, like Fred Lang, even bother to arrest them on the word of a little Chinese girl who didn't even speak English was not as important as the fact that the people of Monterey would know.

His mother would have to disown him, and even that might not be enough to save her reputation. The girl had to disappear, without a trace. And the Irishman with her.

While George weighed his options, he decided he first needed to consult with his mother. He turned on his heels and headed straight for the bank.

Olivia sat in her office and rubbed her forehead.

"We'll discuss why you did it another time. For the present, are you sure she could identify you?"

"The way she looked at me, I'm sure."

Olivia thought for a moment. "I'll talk to Sean. Perhaps he can convince his friend to leave town with the girl. They have no ties here. They could start a new life anywhere."

"And if he can't?"

Olivia paused. "Then, perhaps, Sheriff Lang needs to take her into protective custody, as an eyewitness. Take her to Salinas."

"They hate the Chinese in Salinas."

"Better something happen to her there than in Monterey, if something must happen to her."

Olivia hated even the contemplation of a sad fate for the little girl, but she had to think about her son first -- and her own reputation as well.

An hour later, Olivia and Sean were having dinner at Carmen's.

"So," Olivia began. "How is your friend taking to fatherhood?"

"He seems to enjoy it. Then again, Michael always did like lookin' after people. He's been lookin' after me for all these years."

"And I'm willing to bet you'd probably do anything for one another."

"We're friends," Sean said, matter-of-factly.

144

"Loyalty is important in this world -- especially when it's mutual."

"Mutual loyalty," Sean said, "and mutual trust."

Olivia took a bite of food.

"The little girl is going to need to live near a school, where she can learn English and arithmetic. I hear there's an excellent school for Chinese children up in San Francisco, in their Chinatown."

"I don't know," Sean replied. "Monterey would be more to his likin'. An' he's thinkin' of startin' a store to sell fish the Chinese catch to the non-Chinese."

"Really?" Olivia hesitated, then told him, that "Monterey may not be safe for the little girl any more."

"Why?"

"Rumors are spreading about her," she said softly. "People think she might be able to identify the culprits who killed the Chinese family on the dunes. Perhaps even the culprits have heard the gossip."

"You think they'd come after her?"

"They might. To protect themselves. Of course, Michael could always turn her over to Sheriff Lang for protection."

"Lang? Isn't he a member of that anti-Chinese group?"

She silently responded by not responding.

Sean's mind raced through possible reasons why Olivia would be so concerned, or not so concerned, about Shushu's well-being. Then it hit him.

"Being a parent can be an awful responsibility, I imagine," he said.

Olivia smiled. "Exactly. And I need to know I can trust you, Sean. Especially, if we are to go forward with our real estate venture. You know you can trust me. You can trust me not to tell Sheriff Lang or my older brother, the state senator, about a rumor I heard from a couple of old miners I've known

145

since way back, about a pair of itinerant Franciscan friars who used to travel from mining camp to mining camp, conducting Mass and hearing confessions. One was described to me as a smooth-talking, blonde-haired fellow, with a scarred right cheek, which he tried to hide under a scruffy beard, who had an Irish gift for gab and gave a spirited recitation of the Latin."

Sean kept up his best poker face, as he took another bite of food.

Olivia continued. "They must have taken in quite a lot in donations for the Church -- if they were really doing God's work."

Sean smiled ruefully. "And I would never do anything to bring harm to you or your son, Olivia. Ya' have my word."

Olivia nodded, then held up her glass.

"After all," she said, "we Irish have to stick together."

Sean smiled, then raised his glass to touch hers. "That's how we've survived to this day an' the next."

After which, they both emptied their goblets.

While his mother had her talk with Mulcahy, George Connolly Jr. spent the night drinking with his friends, Billy Clark and Carl Morgan, arguing about what to do about the little Chinese girl.

They had robbed and killed the Zhangs on the spur of the moment, coming across them on their way home after three days of gambling, drinking, and whoring in San Luis Obispo. They couldn't allow a potential eyewitness to remain in their town to identify them.

George told them about his mother's plan to get her new boyfriend to talk his best friend into just going away with his new, adopted daughter, but Billy didn't like it.

"What if they come back?" he asked.

"If your mom does get 'em to leave, we should follow 'em and then ambush 'em outside of town," Carl suggested. "Make it look like highway robbers. Like with the Chinks on the beach."

"It's one thing to kill Chinks," Billy argued. "We blew all our money in San Luis Obispo. Coming across them was fate. We were meant to rob them. But killing a white man, I don't know."

"He's protecting an eyewitness," George said. "The Chinese-lover made his choice. It's them or us."

The next day, Michael invited Ying to accompany him and Shushu on a picnic near the lighthouse at Point Pinos. Ying had been taking more and more time off to spend with the Irishman, but Katy didn't mind. She was a romantic at heart. And the fact they were mixed race couple didn't change her opinion. Katy had a father who was Mexican and a mother who was a member of the Rumsen tribe.

Michael rented a buggy, and Ying collected some Chinese delicacies from Lau's Store, including a box of steamed buns and a package of the paper wrapped sponge cake they all liked so well.

On the way to Point Pinos, they stopped off at the Chinese fishing village to talk to some of the fishermen and their wives about Michael's idea of setting up a shop to sell their fish to the locals. The fishermen, he learned, were organized basically into six family-run companies, so he would have to make deals with each company, which was all right by Michael, but some of the fishermen sought more favorable terms than he was offering the others.

"It's gotta be the same for everyone," Michael said, "or it'll never work. It's all for one, and one for all."

Ying stopped before translating that last part and looked at Michael.

Seeing her expression, he told her, "It's from a book I read a while back," he explained. "Great book."

Ying translated the last part for the fishermen. They looked at Ying, then at Michael, then back at Ying, and finally, at one another.

One of the older, more skeptical wives asked a question, which Ying translated, "She wants to know why do you want to do this for them?"

"Tell her that I'm doin' this for me as much as I'm doin' it for them. No, wait. Tell her that I'm doin' this for me more than I'm doin' it for them. I intend to make 'em money, but I also intend to make money for myself an' my daughter. I've been lookin' for a business to get into, an' this might be it. I know fish. I grew up a fisherman in Ireland. Different ocean. Different kinds of fish. But it's all still fish."

The fishermen and their wives listened intently to the translation, then laughed. It was starting to make sense to them.

George and his friends slept it off in Billy's room in town, then had breakfast at Lyon's Ale Depot and Restaurant. They had resolved to eliminate the Irishman and the little girl. They just needed to find them.

Then, as fate would have it, just as they emerged from Lyon's, they spotted Lonergan diving a rented buggy with the little girl and a Chinese woman toward the Chinese village.

All they had to do was get their horses from the livery stable.

A couple of the women saw the strangers first. White men rarely, if ever, came to the village, and these three did not look the least bit friendly.

148

The women's reactions drew the attention of Michael and Ying, and then Shushu, who turned to see the three white men as they got closer.

The little girl grabbed tightly onto Michael's leg.

At first, he wasn't sure what it was about the intruders that made her afraid, but the hard looks of the young men, as they stared back at Michael and Shushu, gave him a pretty good idea.

As the three men got off their horses, Michael slipped the leather loop off the hammer of his Colt revolver, then removed his spectacles to wipe away any smudges with his handkerchief.

"Are those the men you saw on the dunes?" he asked Shushu.

Ying translated. Shushu nodded, as she continued to clutch onto Michael, as well as her new cloth doll.

Michael put his spectacles back on and watched, as the three young men continued to come closer. They also began to nervously flex their fingers above their holstered guns.

The fishermen and their wives quickly scattered, and Michael motioned for Ying to take Shushu and move away.

"What can I do for you, gentlemen?" Michael asked.

"We want you out of town," Carl shouted out. "We don't take to white people mixing with Chinese."

"I was told there weren't any anti-Chinese feelings in Monterey. Live and let live -- or so I was told."

"So long as they live here, and we live there." Billy pointed back toward Monterey behind him.

"I see. What if my daughter an' I build a house halfway between the two villages?" Michael suggested.

"Don't work that way," George said.

"No middle ground, eh?"

The three men shook their heads.

149

Michael nodded.

George, Carl, and Billy went for their guns, but had barely touched the handles, when Michael had pulled his revolver and was aiming it at them.

His speed surprised and frightened them, more than a little bit. But it also angered them a good deal.

Billy was the first to draw -- or attempt to draw.

Michael shot him in the shoulder, before he could even clear his gun from his holster. The other two ducked for whatever cover they could find.

The Irishman could have easily killed Billy, but he had hoped that by wounding him, they might run away, and he could tell Roberto about them later.

But they had no interest in giving up that quickly. They dropped for cover and returned fire. Billy even retrieved his revolver off the ground, where he had dropped it, and fired with his other hand.

Michael took cover around the corner of one of the houses, which proved much safer than the overturned tables and boxes the young men hid behind. Michael's .45 caliber bullets cut through the boxes and crates, unnerving the trio, who, nonetheless, continued to fire wildly, raising their guns over their cover, without looking where they were aiming.

The fight was not going well for the three friends, and this only served to infuriate the quick-tempered George. He took off his jacket, picked up a piece of dry driftwood, then tied his shirt to it and lit it with a match.

"Cover me!" George called out, then he stood up and tossed the makeshift torch with all his might. It landed in a pile of fishing nets hanging off the building in front of Michael and immediately set them ablaze.

"Now why'd he have to go an' do that?" Michael wondered out loud, then fired off two rounds into the middle of the overturned table George was behind. Both bullets cut through the wood. One of them splintered the wood and cut up his face and ear.

"Damn it!" George cried out, holding his face.

"Are you all right?" Carl asked.

"Keep firing!" George yelled. "Keep firing!"

The three men kept up their fire, repeatedly loading their hand guns from the shells in their gun belts, while the smoke from the burning building made it difficult for Michael to return fire with any accuracy.

Ying and Shushu continued to crouch down behind some crates that the fisherman used to ship their catch to San Francisco. Shushu held her hands over her ears and started to cry. Ying held onto her tightly.

"Quiet, little one," Ying said in Cantonese. "Keep still."

The buildings in the village were all made of driftwood and built close together, which made it easy for the fire to spread quickly.

The villagers watched, as the flames ate away at their homes and wanted to try and put out the fire, but the gunfire made it impossible.

"Michael!" Ying called out. "You've got to end this, before the whole village burns to the ground!"

Michael knew she was right. The building he had been using for cover was being consumed by flames. He could no longer remain there, which was exactly why George had thrown the torch.

As Michael stepped away from the burning building, the three young men stood and opened fire, forcing Michael to dive for cover behind a rack of drying fish, some ten feet from the building. Wood splinters exploded from the rack, raining down on Michael's face and shoulders.

The young men emptied their guns, then ducked back down to reload. Michael wiped the soot and fish scales from his glasses, then made sure his gun was fully chambered.

The Irishman found himself in an awful defensive position, forced to lie on the ground, which was not exactly the best way to fire a handgun -- but there he was, and he had to make the best of it.

"Again!" George shouted, and, again, the three young men blasted away at the same time, gleefully.

Michael listened and counted, as the three men emptied their revolvers, and the moment he heard they had run of out bullets again, he sat up and fired at each of them. He hit both Carl and Billy square in the chest, throwing them back onto the ground, but missed George completely.

George looked over at his two dead friends and lost his will to fight. He holstered his gun, put his jacket back on, crawled back to his horse, and then kept the animal between him and Michael, until he thought he was safe enough away to climb into the saddle and ride off at a gallop.

Michael let him go. He turned his attention to the fire which was consuming the village all around him. He was joined by the fishermen and their wives, who formed a bucket brigade to throw water on the flames.

Smoke from the fishing village could be seen in Monterey even before George had made it back to town. He didn't pause to tell anyone what had happened, not even his mother. He didn't trust Marshal Fuentes to take care of Michael and the little girl. This was a county matter, anyway. He needed to go to Salinas for Sheriff Lang, and his Uncle Walter.

Chapter Twenty-Three

November 7, 1879 -- Monterey

George raced the fourteen miles from Monterey to Salinas to find his uncle and the county sheriff watching Denis Kearney give another one of his rabble-rousing, anti-Chinese stump speeches in the town square.

"And, remember, whatever happens, the Chinese must go!"

The crowd of white faces cheered and applauded eagerly.

George told Walter and Fred about the shootout and Michael killing his two friends -- and how Michael drew first, which, technically, he did, because he was much faster than they were.

Lang immediately called out for volunteers for a posse. The fact they were going after a Chinese-loving white man made it easy. He had more volunteers than he needed right there in the square.

The fire was out of control. The Chinese did what they could, but the buildings were constructed too close together to create a break. The best they could do was try and rescue some of their possessions from their houses, before the flames consumed them.

Michael felt horrible. It wasn't his fault. George threw the makeshift torch. But he still felt in some way responsible.

He worked as hard as any of the Chinese throwing water onto the fire, while Ying and Shushu were part of the bucket brigade, carrying water from the ocean.

George returned to Monterey with his uncle, Sheriff Lang, and a posse of twelve additional men. They didn't really have to, but since they knew Michael was a friend of his, they stopped long enough to inform Marshal Fuentes of their intention to arrest Lonergan for the murders of Billy Clark and Carl Morgan and for Fuentes to keep out of it. This was a county matter.

While Maguire, Lang, and Fuentes talked, the members of the posse bragged to anyone within earshot of how they intended to make an example of the China lover. One of the crowd was Robert Louis Stevenson, on his way back to the hotel after lunch at Lyon's. He quickly deduced the China lover they were talking about was his friend and decided he needed to be warned.

Stevenson found Michael still throwing water on the fire and told him about the racist-bragging posse from Salinas. Michael knew he had to get out of there and take Shushu with him -- and Ying refused to be left behind.

They all climbed into the rented buggy and took off toward the south, but not before relieving Billy and Carl of their gun belts.

Michael knew they wouldn't get far. A horse drawn buggy could not possibly outrun a hard-riding posse. He needed to quickly find a place where they could hole up.

The first location they came across was the ruins of the mission on the Carmel River. It wasn't perfect, but it would have to do.

Shushu was as reluctant to enter the ruined basilica as she had been when Michael and Sean had brought her there on Samhain, but Ying reassured her in Cantonese that it would be all right.

Then they heard the echo of a rattle somewhere in the place.

"Rattlesnake, Michael," Ying called out.

Michael drew his revolver, then stepped carefully through the rubble, listening, as the sound grew louder, and looking for any movement in the dirt that covered the floor.

In the thirty-five years he had lived in the New World, the Irishman had become more accustomed to snakes than he cared to think about. He didn't like them anymore, but he was less frightened of them.

Finally, he found the creature, coiled on the floor, looking up at him, his tongue dancing in and out of his mouth.

Michael pointed his revolver at the snake, then hesitated. While Ying and Shushu watched, Michael holstered his gun, then picked up a tree branch with forked branches at one end. With a cautious, confident jab, he caught the snake just below the head, picked the creature up and walked past the two ladies to one of many openings in the former walls of the basilica, where he flung the snake out onto the field.

He looked back at the astonished Ying and Shushu.

"He wasn't harming anyone," Michael said, simply.

Shushu only scowled. "Shneaky shnaaake."

Ying looked down at the little girl.

"She's already learning English, sort of."

Michael smiled.

The commotion out in the street was an unwanted distraction for the card games being played in the saloon next to the marshal's office, especially for Sean, who had been winning.

Nevertheless, he probably wouldn't have given the riders outside a second look through the window, but he happened to notice Olivia standing near the front, berating her son, who was standing beside his horse.

"What have you done, George?" she asked, with a condescending tone only a mother can lay onto to a son who had disappointed her.

George looked at Olivia, then noticed Sean over her shoulder, approaching them.

"Your friend killed my friends."

"Michael?"

"I told the sheriff -- he killed my friends."

"I told you I would handle it," Olivia said.

"How did it happen?" Sean asked.

"We were minding our own business," George said, spitting out the words, "then he drew on us."

"Michael wouldn't do that."

"Are you calling me a liar?"

Just then, Walter and Fred emerged from the jail and crossed to their horses.

"Sheriff," Sean called out. "Do ya intend to arrest Michael -- or shoot him on sight?"

Lang mounted his horse. "That depends on Lonergan."

Sean looked around at faces of the posse. These were not patient men, interested in giving Michael a chance to surrender. It might spoil their fun.

"What if I go along, Sheriff?" Sean offered. "Talk him into givin' himself up."

Lang looked at Senator Maguire.

"If he can get Lonergan to surrender," Walter whispered, "then we can shoot them both at the same time."

Fred nodded, then looked at Sean. "Get your horse."

Olivia rode with the posse as far as the Chinese fishing village, where they watched the fire consume the houses.

"Well, this'll make it easier to foreclose on the land," Walter said to his sister, before he rode off with the others.

Olivia looked down at the bodies of George's two friends. still lying where they had fallen.

"I didn't want any of this," she whispered sadly.

The posse headed south, following the trail left behind by the wheels of the buggy. It led straight to the old mission.

"He thinks he can hold off all of us from that pile of stones?" one member of the posse wondered out loud, followed by a smug chuckle.

"He did as much, as a younger man," Sean told him.

Lang looked at Sean. "Well?"

Sean took the hint. He rode forward toward the mission, hoping his friend would recognize him.

"Michaleen! Don't shoot!"

Sean entered the courtyard in front of the basilica, then dismounted and walked his horse inside.

"What are you doin' here?" Michael asked.

"I'm here to talk ya into givin' yourself up."

While Ying and Shushu watched, the two men stared at each other for a good five seconds -- before breaking into laughter and hugging one another.

"I can't believe they really fell for that," Sean said with a laugh.

"You shneaky shnaaake!" Michael said.

Shushu ran up and hugged Sean around the legs.

"Uncle Sean," she said. "Ya came. Begorah!"

Sean smiled down at the little girl and tousled her hair.

"Her English is comin' right along. Sounds just like her father."

Michael smiled.

Sean nodded to Ying, as she crossed over and took Shushu by the hand, then he pulled the rifle from his saddle sling and slapped his horse to head off in the direction of a sheltered alcove, where Michael had put the buggy horse.

"Another abandoned Franciscan building, Michaleen. Just like Churubusco."

"I hope not."

Sean laughed, as he and Michael took up firing positions at holes in the north wall and looked out at the posse, who were still mounted.

"I'll take the left wing," Sean suggested. "You take the right. Then we'll work our way toward the middle."

Michael nodded. "Keep 'em bunched."

"That young fella next to the sheriff is Olivia's son. I'd appreciate, if you didn't kill 'im. Olivia'd never forgive me."

"He was one of the fellas that killed the Zhangs. Shushu identified him for me. I got the other two."

"I saw 'em. How'd you miss George?"

"He was my third target," Michael said. "He ducked."

Sean nodded, then looked at the sky. It was beginning to turn twilight orange.

"It's gonna get dark soon enough. We don't wanna do this in the dark."

Michael took off his spectacles and wiped off the smudges, then returned them to his face. "Ready when you are, Seamus."

Sean worked the lever on the repeating rifle he had taken off one of the bandits a few days before, and loaded it carefully as he recited his rhyme.

"In poetry or prose, the San Patricios,
The last remaining of the Wild Geese chose
To make our final stand,
Fallen brothers close at hand,
We, last of all the San Patricios!"

Sean took aim and opened fire.

The man on the far west side of the row of horsemen grabbed his chest and fell off his mount. A moment later, the man on the east side also hit the ground. The rest of the posse quickly got off their horses, but not before two more men were shot.

"That knocks the odds down some," Sean said, with a laugh, while firing another round.

The eleven remaining members of the posse took cover and returned a blistering fire, cutting chunks out of the walls of the mission.

The two ladies hid behind an overturned, heavy wooden pew. Shushu began to cry out, clutching her cloth doll and screaming "Stop!" over and over again.

"Not to worry, little sprite," Michael said, trying to calm her. "Uncle Sean an' me used to do this for a livin'."

Ying cradled Shushu in her arms and covered the little one's body with hers.

"Were you ever shot?" Ying asked.

"Oh sure," Sean replied, while reloading his rifle. "At the second battle of Angostura."

"Second battle?" Ying asked.

"Aye. But since then, we've tried to keep our injuries to a minimum."

Moments later, a bullet ripped loose a chunk from the wall, which then hit Sean in the middle of the "D" on his right cheek.

"Damn it to bloody hell!"

"Don't swear in front of Shushu!" Michael told him.

Sean looked over at the little girl.

"Sorry, little one. My own fault. Never tempt fate in a house of God by braggin' about how lucky you've been in battle."

As fire was returned back and forth, Michael noticed the posse trying to move around the sides of the building.

"They're tryin' to flank us," he said.

Sean took aim and shot the posse member furthest to their left, while Michael fired twice to hit the man furthest on the right.

"Took ya two, Michaleen."

"That's okay. I got plenty o' shells. An' there're only nine of 'em left."

The remaining members of the posse continued to empty their repeating rifles, aiming at the holes in the building from which the two Irishmen were picking them off. And the posse's aim was getting better.

Moments later, Michael took a bullet in his right shoulder.

"Owww!"

"Michael!" Ying cried out.

"Stay back!"

"Not to worry," Sean said. "The hole will match the one in his left shoulder. Got that during a poker game, right, Michaleen?"

"You oughta know. He was aimin' at you." Michael replied, as he stuck a bandana into the bullet hole, "which is why we never sit next to one another playin' poker any more."

As Michael reloaded his revolver, Sean moved to a new position in the crumbling wall, peered out and said, "They're movin' closer."

"Easier to hit that way," Michael answered back.

Just then, a bullet cut through the wall and struck Sean in his left shoulder.

"Damn it to hell!" he called out.

Michael looked over at his friend.

"What?" Sean said. "I didn't say 'bloody'."

Ying told Shushu to stay where she was, then crawled across the floor to where Michael had left Billy and Carl's gun belts. She drew the one that had belonged to Carl Morgan and pointed it through a crevice in the wall.

"Do you know how to use that?" Sean asked.

"Three is better than two," Ying angrily replied, pulled back the hammer, and fired.

"I like her!" Sean exclaimed loudly. "But don't shoot the Connolly boy."

Shushu had had quite enough of the noise. She crawled out from behind the heavy wooded pew and made her way next to Michael.

"Yeh Yeh! Yeh Yeh!"

"Shushu! Get back behind the pew!" Michael told her, harshly.

Just then, a bullet tore in through the wall behind them and struck the heavy wooden pew Shushu had been hiding behind.

"One of 'em got behind us!" Michael called out, then looked down at Shushu. "Aren't you the clever one. How'd you know he'd done that, little sprite?"

He kissed her on top of her head, then looked over at Sean.

"Which one of us let him outflank us?"

Sean got to his feet. "I'll ask him."

Sean quickly made his way to the other side of the church, then peered out through a crack in the wall.

A solitary rifleman was crouched down on one knee, firing his Winchester repeating rifle back at him.

"Cheeky bastard," Sean said to himself.

As Sean worked the lever on his Winchester rifle, a bullet found its way through a large hole in the wall and struck Sean just above his right hip.

"Oww!" he exclaimed. "Damned anti-papist!"

Sean quickly raised the rifle to his right shoulder and fired off a round.

The shot missed the rifleman, but he reacted as if the bullet may have passed by his right ear. So, Sean worked the lever on his rifle, then adjusted his aim ever so slightly and fired again. The second shot hit the rifleman on the bridge of his nose.

Sean suddenly needed to take a moment to catch his breath. He leaned against one of the broken pews and removed the bandana from around his neck to jam it into the bleeding hole in his shoulder, then pulled up his shirt and undershirt, to get a look at wound just above his right hip.

There was no way to apply a tourniquet, so he removed the bandana from his shoulder, and jammed it into the new wound. It would just have to do for the time being.

As he slowly made his way back to the other side of the church, Sean looked around at the ruins and the remnants of religious decoration, faded or broken, but still glistening in the orange glow of the twilight sun as it seeped through the various gaps in the church's walls and ceiling. Sean crossed himself and said a silent prayer. It would soon be dark.

Chapter Twenty-Four

November 7, 1879 -- Monterey

As Sean returned to his firing position on the north wall, a bullet struck Michael, cutting into his left hand, causing him to drop his gun.

"Bloody hell!"

At that moment, Ying was the only one returning fire, and she wasn't much of a shot.

"Ying," Michael said. "Take Shushu an' hide in the sacristy."

"The what?"

"That room back there. Sean an' I are swearin' far too much for her to stay here."

Ying looked at Michael, then picked up Carl Morgan's gun belt, with an ample supply of bullets fixed along the back, and slung it over her shoulder.

"Come along, Shushu," Ying said in Cantonese.

"No!" the little one said in her brogue-tinged English. "I want ta stay!"

"Go with Ying, little sprite. Everything'll be all right."

He kissed her again on the top of the head, then gave Shushu's hand to Ying, who led her back to the sacristy, crouching all the way.

Sean paused for a moment to hold his side.

"Lyin' to your daughter already, Michaleen?"

"Granddaughter."

"Granddaughter?"

"Long story."

Michael looked over at his friend and noticed him breathing heavily.

"You all right?"

Sean looked to see that Ying and Shushu were out of earshot.

"Bastard shot me in the hip."

"Same hip?"

"No. The other. Now both hips are gonna hurt, when it rains."

"I'm sure it wasn't intentional," Michael said. "Unless he's the one that shot you at Churubusco."

"Didn't recognize him," Sean replied.

Soon enough, the posse realized the people in the mission had stopped firing at them. Cautiously, they got to their feet and moved in toward their target. They knew the cease fire might easily be a feint to get them to come closer and make them easier targets.

Michael picked up his revolver in his right hand and slowly forced the hammer back with his bloody left fingers.

"They're comin'."

Sean sat up and checked his revolver.

The posse continued their slow approach, some of them firing, while others reloaded their rifles or hand guns.

Fred smiled. "Just like old times, eh, Walter?"

Walter sighed. "Yeah."

"Don't worry, ole buddy. I'll finish 'em off. You won't even have to get your hands dirty. That's my job."

Fred looked around at the rest of the posse. "You guys wait out here. The senator and I will go in alone."

"I wanna go in," George said.

"You stay here," Walter told his nephew.

"Leave this to the experienced professionals, boy," Fred added.

Sean and Michael watched carefully through the crevices in the walls. They knew they would have to wait until the last moment.

"How's your stomach?" Michael asked.

Sean smiled, then doubled over, while Michael leaned back against some rubble. He took off his spectacles to wipe off the smudges, but only succeeded in making them worse, smearing one of the lenses with blood. Nevertheless, he returned them to his face. At least, he could still see through the other lens, more or less.

After what seemed like an eternity, Fred and Walter appeared at the entrance and walked up to Michael.

"Where's the little girl?" Fred asked.

"I left her in the fishin' village, where she'll be safe."

"The fishing village?"

"All Chinese look alike to ya, don't they?"

The sheriff kicked Michael in his hand, sending the revolver he was holding skittering across the floor and causing him to cry out in pain.

"Let's try this again."

Walter walked over to get a closer look at Sean. "Finish him off, Fred. I want to get home, before it's too late."

As usual, Walter telling him what to do, irritated Fred.

"I know my job," he said, looking at the senator.

"So do I," Michael said, and pulled Billy Clark's revolver he had hidden under his leg and shot the sheriff,

165

clean through the head, the bullet entering under his chin and exiting through the top of his skull.

Walter looked back to see Fred's dazed, empty expression, then watched his old friend fall to the floor.

That gave Sean a chance to sit up and empty his own revolver into Walter's chest. The senator collapsed in a bloody heap.

"Took ya six," Michael said.

Sean emptied the casings from his gun, then reloaded it as quickly as his broken and bloody hands would let him.

"Had to use my left hand. I wanted to make sure."

Michael crawled over to retrieve his Colt that Fred had kicked out of his hand. As shot up as they were, they were determined to give the posse as good a defense as they could muster.

Just then, they heard the sound of more horses. Sean looked out a hole in the wall and saw another group of riders arriving from Monterey.

"Looks like they got reinforcements," Sean said.

"Bloody hell. I hope we got enough bullets."

The new group of about twenty or so rode up to the posse and pointed their guns at them.

"What's that all about?" Michael wondered.

Sean smiled. "Clean your glasses, Michaleen. It's Bob!"

"Bob? Can a city marshal's posse stop a county sheriff's posse?"

"They can, if they out number them three to one!"

"Inside the mission! It's Marshal Fuentes! I'm coming in!"

Roberto walked in carefully, not exactly sure who was still alive and who wasn't.

"Well, you two look the worse for wear."

"I suppose it's a crime in California to kill a county sheriff and a state senator," Sean said, "even in self-defense."

Roberto paused for a moment. "Not if they shot each other."

Roberto grabbed Fred by the collar and dragged him closer to Walter, to make his theory of a shootout between the two appear slightly more plausible, then kicked a little dirt over the blood trail Fred's body had left behind.

"They were always fighting about one thing or another. It's always a shame, when two old *compañeros de armes* have a falling out."

Just then, Ying and Shushu returned from the sacristy and hurried over to attend to Michael's shoulder.

Sean smiled. "Nice to have a family to look after ya in your old age, Michaleen."

Michael smiled.

Dr. Heintz, the town doctor, who had accompanied Marshal Fuentes's posse, entered the basilica and crossed over to Sean, followed by Father Lucien, who paused to look at the bullet holes in the walls.

"Heaven preserve us," the father said, half aloud, half in prayer.

"Sorry, Father," Michael said, as he slipped his Colt .45 back into his holster. "I guess posses in California don't respect the concept of church sanctuary."

"Well, I shall have to have a talk with them about that," the indignant Franciscan declared.

"At least you can now prove to Mrs. Faulkner just how sturdy these walls really are," Sean added.

"George Connolly was one of the fellas that killed the Zhangs," Michael told Roberto.

"I know," the marshal replied. "I just arrested him for selling stolen property. Lazy bastard couldn't even be bothered to go to Salinas or Watsonville to try and sell Madame Zhang's jade necklace."

"Don't swear in front of my granddaughter, Bob."

"Sorry, Miguelito," Roberto said, with a smile.

Michael removed his spectacles and handed them to Shushu. "Clean those for me, will you, little sprite?"

Shushu smiled, then set down her cloth doll and wiped the lenses with one of the new handkerchiefs Michael had bought her the day before.

Meanwhile, Michael motioned for Ying to come in closer -- and gave her a kiss on the lips.

"I was wondering when you would get around to that," she said, then kissed him back, before returning to dressing his shoulder wound.

"What do you look like, clean shaven?" Ying asked.

"Not sure I remember."

Ying whispered something into Shushu's ear. The little girl looked up at Michael, then nodded.

"You, too, little sprite?"

Shushu smiled, then handed her *Yeh Yeh* back his clean spectacles.

"How'd ya get so many townspeople to help rescue a couple strangers?" Sean asked Roberto.

"I told them you two were the last of the San Patricios," Roberto replied. "At its heart, Monterey is still a Mexican pueblo, and we remember our heroes."

"Really?"

"Two of the fellows out there had grandfathers at Churubusco."

"Grandfathers?"

Roberto nodded.

Sean sighed. "So many grandfathers and grandchildren about nowadays."

Dr. Heintz looked up. "Marshal. This man is badly wounded. We need to get him back to town."

Father Lucien helped the doctor carry Sean to the buckboard, in which the two men had ridden out to the mission. Father Lucien stayed by Sean's side as the doctor drove his buckboard back to town. Concerned by Sean's labored breathing, Father Lucien leaned close to Sean's ear and softly asked, "Would you like me to give you your last rites, my son?"

"Not to worry, Father. I've been shot up worse than this before," Sean replied. "But I've been thinkin' I might like to make my confession. Do you have time?"

Father Lucien smiled and answered, "I do, if you do."

In that moment, thinking of all his transgressions, and how long it would take to list them all, Sean laughed, then howled in pain.

Seeing the mournfully compassionate look on Father Lucien's face, Sean squeezed his eyes shut, to keep from laughing again.

As Father Lucien began reciting The Lord's Prayer, he felt Sean's firm grip on his arm. Looking down, he saw the Irishman look back up at him with a pained smile.

"I'd prefer ya recite something in Latin, if you don't mind. I like the Latin."

THE END

AFTERWORD

In the San Jacinto Plaza in the San Angel District of Mexico City, there hangs a commemorative plaque, placed there in 1969, which translates "In memory of the Irish soldiers of the St. Patrick's Battalion, martyrs, who gave their lives to the Mexican cause in the United States unjust invasion of 1847."

The history and heroism of the San Patricios during the Mexican-American War from 1846 to 1848 has been very well documented in several books by several authors. What became of the very few survivors is mostly a matter of conjecture and speculation.

This novel is a work of fiction, set in the very real world of Mexico and the American West in the Nineteenth Century. Sean Mulcahy and Michael Lonergan are not based on real people, though many of the characters they come across in Mexico and Monterey were real, including John Riley, the commanding officer of the San Patricios, and Robert Louis Stevenson, who had spent the last months of 1879 in Monterey on his way to San Francisco. Other characters, such as Father Lucien du Montfort and Mrs. Alice Faulkner, are fictionalized versions of their real-life counterparts: Father Angel Casanova and Mrs Charles Crocker.

Certainly, and most unfortunately, the anti-Irish, anti-Catholic prejudice of the 1840s and 1850s and the anti-Chinese prejudice of the 1870s, 1880s, and into the Twentieth Century, were also very real.

The large number of Irish and German Catholics coming to the U.S. in the 1840s led anti-immigrant, anti-papist, native Americans to form a number of secret organizations, such as the Order of the Star Spangled Banner in 1849, which grew into the American political party, also known as the "Know-Nothings," because they repeatedly refused to tell outsiders what they stood for. Bloody and violent riots that occurred in Philadelphia, New York, Baltimore, and Louisville, Kentucky did their talking for them.

As for the Chinese, the United States Congress passed the Page Act in 1875, which banned Chinese females from immigrating to the United States alone. This was followed up by the Chinese Exclusion Act of 1882, which banned the immigration of Chinese laborers, which remained in effect until it was partially repealed by the Magnuson Act of 1943, and was only fully repealed by the Immigration and Nationality Act of 1965.

The fire at the fishing village on Point Alones actually occurred on November 9, 1899, when a rubbish pile caught fire and burned about 75% of the village. There were subsequent fires in 1898, 1902, and a final fire in 1906, which happened during eviction negotiations between the Chinese fishermen and the Pacific Improvement Company, who owned the land. The Chinese were not allowed to rebuild.

Made in the USA
San Bernardino, CA
28 July 2020

76179044R00102